A STOLEN PRINCESS...

Two struggling men came into Yamin's view. One, by the torn hem of his paso and the tangled twist of his turban, was a ruffian, but the other...!

Yamin sat up straighter and bumped his head on his puppet basket top.

The man was big. A giant, surely. With hair the color of dusty rice, and clothed in two tubes that held his legs and a dusty jacket. They fought over something small and glittering.

Minthamee! The princess puppet, her creamy longyi and blouse covered in jewels. The small jeweled pins fell out of her hair and her hair fell loose in a raven cascade of softness. They could rip out her hair! They could break her limbs!

He went to shove open his basket to help her, but the small ruffian gave up and bolted out of the mess of baskets. The giant man straightened Minthamee's longyi and stroked her hair—a total affront, even if the man's handling was gentle. He murmured something Yamin didn't understand.

Then a familiar shout came from a direction he couldn't see. The puppeteers came running, and the dust-haired giant turned and ran for his horse, Minthamee still in his hands.

Fantasy and Mystery by Karen L. Abrahamson

Mystery (Writing as K.L. Abrahamson)
Through Dark Water

Fantasy Mystery
Aung and Yamin Series
Death By Effigy (Guardbridge Books)
A Death in Passing
Death In Umber

The Cartographer Universe
(in chronological order)
The Warden of Power
Impossible
The Cartographer's Daughter
The American Geological Survey Series:
Afterburn
Aftershock
Aftermath
Afterimage
Terra Incognita
Terra Infirma
Terra Nueva

Other Fantasy Novels
Ice Dragon
Emberstone
Mutable Things
The Crystal Courtesan

Death In Umber

Karen L. Abrahamson

Death
In
Umber

Chapter 1

The afternoon sun placed a heavy weight on Aung's shoulders, though his step was lighter than it might have been, for he carried only the weight of guilt instead of a physical burden. Under a cloudless blue sky he led the royal puppet troupe—keepers of the magical *yoke thei*, the eighteen-inch-tall Yamani-wood puppets—in a straggling procession along the narrow road past red-brick stupa, the twenty-foot-spires that dotted the dry plains like some kind of mushroom.

Occasionally he stepped off into dry grass or thorny ditches when one of the great, two-wheeled water wagons trundled past. The dun-colored oxen strained and sweated from the load of huge red urns filled with river water for the farms sprinkled amongst the stupa. The man-high wagon wheels and the puppet troupe's tired feet raised clouds of red dust that stained clothing and skin. Even the youngest apprentice, the singer Thura, had a red face creased with lines like an old man. The dust got into everything and tasted of mud and iron.

The road swung in a sharp curve around one of the mighty red brick *pahtos*—the temples that overshadowed the numerous smaller stupa. Indeed, many of the small spires sprouted as far as Aung could see across the red earth plain, for this was Pagan, the remains of a great kingdom that had—for some mysterious reason—vanished into history. What had once been a great civilization had left behind only this huge plain along the river, dotted with more spires and temples than anyone could count. Most were abandoned, but the largest of the temples were still used by the farmers and villagers who lived among them.

Perhaps they were the descendants of those who built this once-mighty place.

Aung stopped for a moment and looked back at the troupe. He alone of them was not burdened by one of the large wicker trunks that carried their precious *yoke thei* or the weight of the gong circle or the mighty carved dragon that carried the dragon drum. Even seventeen-year-old Thura was burdened by the pack of bamboo poles that would become the puppet stage and the wicker trunk that carried their curtains. And Saya Lin, their troupe leader, who had seen nearly the same sixty years as Aung, still carried the trunk of the Thagyar Min—the celestial king puppet.

The fact that Aung was not physically burdened was the greatest burden of all as he watched Saya Lin stumble and his friends struggle in the heat. But Aung was the eldest and over the past years his age had sapped his strength so that he no longer carried a burden—instead he had become a burden himself—or at least it felt so.

"Old friend, let me help you," Aung asked. "Let me carry your trunk for a time so that you can rest."

Saya Lin's tired gaze flashed up to him. "A puppeteer who cannot carry his puppet must retire. You know that as well as I. Now get out of my way."

Aung caught his arm. "Then perhaps we should rest for a while. Perhaps until evening. It will be cooler then."

Saya Lin ripped free and shoved past, no longer quite the old friend that Aung had known almost all his life. Aung stood there as the rest of the troupe shuffled past, leaving only Aung and faithful Thura beside him.

Aung and wiry-limbed Saya Lin had apprenticed together. They had become journeymen at their crafts— Saya Lin as a puppeteer and Aung as a singer. They had performed together over many years until they were masters of their arts and known and revered across all of Burma and perhaps beyond. But things had changed these past six months. The king still suffered their patronage, but for how long they didn't know. The murder of their Min puppet, the effigy of the human king, had left them a flawed troupe, and when the king got wind of it, he would surely withdraw his patronage. If he learned that they had been so flawed even during their recent royal performances—well, who could say what kind of revenge the king would wreak?

Now, after Aung's insistence had led them to a nearly disastrous visit to the home of the king of the nats, the spirits, he was insisting again. This time, at the request of the king of the spirits and against Saya Lin's wishes, Aung was leading them again, this time to the troubled south and the city of Yangoon.

"He is just tired, Master. It is a long, hot journey I had hoped not to take again," Thura said. He was so young, and straight-backed and with a voice so sweet, Aung had insisted he be his apprentice, even though the lad had been born to the Chin Hills people. He wore his blue *paso*—his sarong—with the front panel pulled up between his legs and tucked into his waistband to allow the air around his ankles. A vest and light cotton shirt protected his back and shoulders from the pack he carried.

Aung nodded. "He bears great burdens as our manager and leader. It is more than a puppeteer should have to carry, but someone had to assume that task."

He set out after the troupe with Thura at his heels, feeling the weight of the sun and of his decisions, for truly he was responsible for the growing schism between himself and Saya Lin.

After their escape from the king's palace in Amarapura, it was Aung who had insisted on visiting Mount Popa—to near fatal results for some of the troupe. He was also the one who had made a deal with the King of the Nats. In return for the mighty spirit king, Min Mahagiri, assuming some of Aung's burden of age, Aung would continue to seek ways to keep the old faith present in the people's lives and would solve the mysteries that clouded justice. The first task Min Mahagiri had set was to travel to Yangoon. Saya Lin had not been happy, for it was Saya Lin's job as leader to determine their travels and Yangoon was best avoided, for it was dangerous with too many foreigners about.

But Yangoon was many days' journey overland through country that would parch a man, so now they traveled to Pagan town in hopes of hiring a boat to take them down the length of the Ayeyarwady River.

Beside them, the huge dark bulk of a pahto grew up out of the earth like a boil upon the plain. Above the tops of the dusty htaung trees with their twisted branches, seven great tiers of brick lifted into the sky in a sullen pyramid, surmounted by a giant corncob-shaped pinnacle. On each step, three great vacant doorways yawned blackness into the day as if they screamed rage or pain or...

Aung didn't know. But this was a haunted place. The people who lived here might venture into such a place to pray at the ancient Buddha images, but it was not for him. Not, as far as he was concerned, for anyone living.

Ahead, the troupe seemed to avert their faces from the pahto. Aung did the same. Just let them get to the river, leave behind this haunted place and the ills that had befallen them. In the south, in Yangoon, surely it would not be as inhospitable. They would just need to be careful.

Just past the narrow, walled lane that led to the temple's walled courtyard, a thicket of htaung trees and thorn brush offered shade from the sun. Saya Lin threw off his burden with a groan and sank down onto the ground beside his trunk.

"It is too hot. We should rest here for the afternoon and continue our march in the cooler evening," he said.

"But that's what you..." Thura started.

Aung grabbed his arm to stop him. "He is our leader. It is up to him to decide."

The other troupe members settled their precious bundles to the earth and slumped down beside them. Thura and round-faced Zeya, the apprentice puppeteer, gathered kindling from under the trees and brought it to broad-shouldered Nyein, the dragon drummer. He lit a fire and readied a small pot to boil rice for a lunchtime meal.

It was a dusty place and Aung listened to the hoo-hoo, hoo-hoo of the ghostly gray doves and the wind fluting in the doors and windows of the darkened temple. As the moments ticked past, he felt the shadow of the huge structure creep across the dusty fallen walls and dry fields toward them. In the rainy season, this field would grow in the midst of all this desolation—he could see the furrows of last year's oxen-drawn plows crisscrossing the dirt—but now it was a desert of brown scrub grass between the lines of withered trees.

Soon the fire burned merrily and the pot of water steamed. Aung stood to ease his back and step beyond the huge structure's reach. His tired troupe mates talked quietly and dozed on the ground. Thura and Zeya had wandered farther down the road, apparently forgetting the trouble that had befallen them when they went exploring not so long ago. Aung glanced up at the omnipresent temple with its huge doorways and cracked and crumbling niches that might once have held something more.

Something moved in one of the doorways on the second tier of the temple.

Startled, he looked more closely. This was more than a bird. Surely he had seen something—a flash of umber?—in one of the doorways.

He stepped closer to the narrow road leading to the temple courtyard and the tall, carved lintels that guarded the entrance. Surely something stirred in that black maw of the main entrance and for a moment he thought of a tongue, unfolding swiftly enough to catch them and draw them in like some immense lizard.

He jerked back a step at the image, just as a pink-clad person stumbled out of the darkness. A shaven head gleamed in the sunlight. A nun, for only Buddhist nuns shaved their heads and wore the pink robes. She turned to the roadway and must have spotted Aung, for she raised her arm and called to him. Then she sank to her knees and collapsed face forward onto the ground.

Aung stood frozen. What had just happened?

"Did you see?" he asked, in case it was his imagination. In this strange place it was possible he had not seen what he thought. He turned to steady-headed U Myint, who had come up beside him. U Myint had the high cheekbones of his Kachin grandfather's clan from near Myitkyina. He had the strong arms and shoulders of a puppeteer but his eyes were sad. His garuda puppet had been one of those lost in the debacle in Amarapura and he still mourned his small charge.

"A nun," U Myint said.

"She's collapsed," Aung called as he hurried toward her. Dust rose around his feet in a thick red cloud. A slight breeze swirled the dirt into his eyes and they were streaming by the time he knelt at the woman's side.

She lay face down in the dirt as if prostrating herself, her pink robes pulled around her, her small feet poking out from the hem, both shoulders bared where the fold of her robe had slipped when she fell. He hesitated to touch her, for it was not proper to touch a nun, but finally he caught her hand.

"Sister? Sister?"

He patted the back of her hand and her fingers shifted. She groaned and stirred in the dust and turned her face toward him.

Young. Very young, by the smooth skin of her thin face. Her eyes widened and she yanked her hand away and fumbled up to sitting, settling her robes across her shoulder again, just as Saya Lin and the others rushed to Aung's side.

Her dark gaze skittered from Aung to those behind him as she swayed and swallowed. Her face was thin, the skin almost translucent over bone as if she had not seen a full meal in a long while. Was that why she had collapsed?

"You." Her voice was soft and musical—someone Aung would like to hear sing. "You are them—the king's own puppet troupe."

Aung frowned and glanced back at Saya Lin. The old puppeteer stepped forward. "We are the Royal Yoke Thei."

"How did you know to come here?" she asked. Her voice had grown stronger even as her face grew puzzled.

"We are on our way from Mount Popa to the river," Aung said. "We are going to Yangoon." He heard Saya Lin stir behind him and knew his old friend's expression would have twisted.

She nodded. "I heard what happened at the festival. The pahtos and trees ring with the story the pilgrims tell of the puppeteers who solved a mystery and brought justice out of evil. Have you come to do the same here?"

There was an eager spark in the nun's dark gaze that sent a shiver of fear up Aung's back. What had they walked into?

He glanced up at Saya Lin again and watched the situation register in the hardening of Saya Lin's mouth.

"What has happened, Sister?" Aung asked just as Saya Lin said, "We are traveling through to the river."

The young nun looked from one to the other. "There is—trouble. Please help us."

She climbed to her feet, swayed a moment, but steadied. "Come, please." She turned toward the gaping entrance to the temple.

Aung hesitated, half-formed premonitions placing a light sweat upon his skin. Carved into the stone on either side of the door, where the effigy of the nat Min Mahagiri usually greeted visitors, lay ravaged places where someone had chiseled out the image. In anger? Doing the king's bidding to drive away the nats? The spirits of the land who brought good harvests and luck to homes had long been part of Burmese Buddhist beliefs, but the king had recently ordered the people to stop believing because he thought good karma would come to a country of purer Buddhism. The orders had led to a schism between the nats and those who listened to the king's orders. This defacing would anger the great nat, Min Mahagiri.

Aung shivered. This was—not a good place. At least not good for him. Farther along the stone wall were a series of beautifully carved Jataka stones that told the story of Buddha's life. At least that was right.

Sending a prayer to Buddha and to Min Mahagiri, he followed.

After the heat of the sun, stepping into the darkness was akin to diving into the deep pools of Inle Lake when he was a boy. Darkness enveloped him and, just as with the lake, glimmering shadows and secret streamers of light cut through the gloom to light a Buddha face in front of him and faded paintings on the wall. The scent of new incense filled his nose, and as his eyes adjusted, he made out a marigold-garlanded brazier set before a twenty-foot-high seated Buddha figure. To either side ran long, high-ceilinged corridors called ambulatories that ran the width of the building just inside the outer walls. The ambulatories would turn to continue on inside the square base of the huge temple.

The Buddha image was white-faced and serene, but the air around it seemed to quiver—in fear?

"This way," the nun hurried along the tall ambulatory that skirted the immense, inner mass of the pahto that would have been built to hold safe a holy relic of Buddha or another holy teacher. The curved ceiling towered above them, plaster still holding the remains of brilliant murals lost in the shadows. Their breath echoed as they followed after the swishing pink robes of the nun as she almost ran down the great avenue. Underfoot the stone was dusty and laced with footprints.

At the end of the ambulatory, where it turned down the next long side of the temple, the nun stepped to the outer wall and disappeared. When Aung arrived at the spot, he found a small stairwell had been constructed in a cunningly built fold in the wall. The stairwell drilled up through the brick until, high above, streamers of light lit the red stone as if from within.

Aung ducked into the tight space and trudged up the stairs, his troupe mates following. Up and up, his old legs protesting at the abuse as the stairwell turned and turned again. It was doubtful that he could have even made the climb if Min Mahagiri had not assumed the weight of some of Aung's long years. The passage was narrow enough that he scraped red dust onto his white shirt's shoulders before he reached the top where the stairs spat him out onto another platform. Another broad ambulatory stretched the length of this level of the temple. Shadows and whispers of the wind and something else slid through the shadowy ceilings, avoiding the light spilling into the hallway through the three open doors that illuminated more seated Buddha figures. They serenely surveyed the countryside. He'd seen someone move in one of those doorways.

The nun was halfway down the ambulatory and motioned back at him to follow as she steadied herself against the wall.

He hurried after her, down the long passage, with the wind cooled by the heights and the darkness so his sweat dried on his body. Another corner and the passage continued, more doors to the outside allowing in bright columns of light. More Buddha figures serenely peering out as if to bless the parched countryside. Here, Buddha's goodness had faded, but then Buddha was not a god, only a learned man. So the figures peered over the countryside providing guidance to those who lived in this parched place:

All is suffering. Everything passes away. Ergo, this suffering, too, will pass.

Aung could almost reassess his feelings about the place. Strange, yes. But grand. And sad, and comforting in a strange way. What a place it would have been when it was newly painted and in use.

Halfway down this length of the ambulatory in one of the dark places between the Buddha figures, another nun stood waiting.

The young nun panted up to her and together they faced Aung and the others. Then Aung realized that it was not just the two nuns he faced. There was a third figure, but this one was clad in umber robes and lay huddled like a sleeping dog up against the base of the ambulatory wall.

Aung went to his knees beside the curled form.

Young—very young. Really no more than a child. A novice monk, then, for he wore the umber robes of the monk in training just as Aung had done so many years ago. Sons were sent to study with local monasteries across Burma. The children learned to read and write and the Buddhist scriptures and monastic way of life before they were either released back to their parents or decided to continue with their studies. Most were young rascals who spent their time finding ways to break the monastery rules and were certainly never far from trouble.

This young lad had apparently found the ultimate trouble.

"He is dead," said the nun who had awaited their arrival.

Aung glanced up at her. She was old—much older than the nun who had led them here, though apparently not as spent as the young nun who still breathed heavily after her climb back into the temple. The elder nun's face was a skein of lines, her eyes two bright pebbles that caught the light, her mouth a crinkled maw of red from chewing betel. She had bony shoulders and arms twisted with old muscle. For all her apparent age, she stood straight-backed with no sign of infirmity.

"What happened?" Aung asked. Saya Lin nodded beside him.

The old nun shook her head. "I do not know," she said in a voice that creaked like stiff leather. "Saw Nang and I came to change the flowers today, just as we do every week. We found him here like this." She shook her head.

Saya Lin knelt beside Aung and together they leaned over the small curled form. His knees were bent as if he curled into himself. His small hands were claws as if he'd fought with someone. His mouth was open, as were his eyes. They had gone milky as if they looked beyond the darkness. Was he terrified as he awaited his next life? Had he made the passage to a better place or was he destined to become a hungry ghost?

Aung shook himself. This was a child. Perhaps this early death was penance for ill deeds in a past life. Something ill had been done to him to rebalance the karmic wheel.

"Look at his throat," Saya Lin murmured.

Time had allowed deep black bruises to form.

"Strangled, then," Aung said.

"But who would strangle a child?" Thura asked from among the other puppeteers.

Aung shook his head. "Who can say. It is an ill thing. An ill thing indeed."

He stood and gave Saya Lin a hand up. Both of their knees crackled and popped.

"Where is he from?" Aung asked. "They will need to be notified and the culprit found."

The two nuns looked at each other.

"But are you not the royal puppet troupe recently at Popa? We heard of you from pilgrims returning from the festival. Saw Nang spotted you on the road and I sent her to call you. I am Daw Ma Kyi, Abbess of our small community." She placed her palms together before her face and bowed to Aung.

He and Saya Lin copied her movements, for as abbess she was a learned woman, deserving of such deference.

"We dance the royal yoke thei," Saya Lin allowed, naming the famous royal puppets that were, unbeknownst to royals and commoners alike, also inhabited by magical nats, the remnants of the spirit of the great Yamani tree from which the puppets were carved.

Daw Ma Kyi looked from one to the other of the old men as if she was waiting. Then she looked beyond them to the others of the troupe. "I was told you investigated another death and brought the killer to justice. Is that not true?"

Aung cringed, for though he had revealed the true killer, it was the nats who brought the justice they thought the culprit deserved. It had not been pretty, and he had been troubled by his role in naming the killer. What if he'd been wrong?

He glanced at Saya Lin, whose expression had turned grim.

"The investigation was forced upon us when it affected the troupe," Aung finally ventured. "We are not investigators."

But the young body curled on the cold stone deserved better than this death. He should be rascaling through Pagan town. He should be laughing. Instead the cool breeze in the ambulatory was the only breath past his lips, the only sigh.

"We can at least help remove the body," Aung said. "He cannot stay here." He looked to Saya Lin, who finally nodded and then motioned to U Myint. U Myint had always been a steady, trustworthy fellow and since the loss of his garuda puppet he had worked hard to make himself useful. When other puppeteers might have become mired in despair at the loss of their "little brother," U Myint had kept his grief in check and assumed other tasks wherever he could.

"Bring the body," Saya Lin said.

Then he turned and left, the remaining puppet troupe members straggling after him. Aung and U Myint watched them leave, then turned back to Daw Ma Kyi and Saw Nang.

"Before we move him, let me look around a moment," said Aung. "This was where the boy was found? He was not moved?" He once more knelt beside the small body.

"We checked to see if he was alive, but otherwise we did not move him," Daw Ma Kyi said.

"Was he lying like he is now, or in some other position?" For the boy appeared to be huddled against the wall as if he'd cowered there. Or perhaps had been dropped?

He glanced up at the nuns.

"I think he was just like that," Saw Nang said. Daw Ma Kyi nodded.

Aung glanced at the bruises on the boy's neck and up at the wall. There were fresh scratch marks across the ancient paintings on the stone. Dropped, then. The killer had the young monk by the neck pressed against the wall and then dropped the body when the deed was done. The question was why.

The wind whispered answers as it dusted along the floor. He stood up, old joints creaking no matter that Min Mahagiri had relieved him of some of age's pain. He nodded at U Myint, who gently gathered up his small burden.

"We will help you take him to his monastery," Aung said.

The two nuns looked at each other again. "We have matters we must take care of here, first," Daw Ma Kyi said. "It is our fortune to provide incense and flowers to this temple's Buddha."

He noted then the two baskets abandoned farther down the tunnel and the faint perfume of marigolds in the air. "Then we will take the body down with us and pray that you join us when you have finished your task." He bowed and started back the way he'd come, U Myint following with the body.

Behind he heard the hushing sweep of the nun's robes against the stone and then their soft voices as they set about their business.

Through the broad arched doorways, the breeze carried the heat and dust of midday and for a moment

Aung regretted that he would be leaving the cool confines of the temple. At the corner he stepped into the stairwell, just as a shout of alarm came from outside. The premonition of disaster sent him stumbling down the stairs.

Chapter 2

The lifting of the lid of his wicker basket disturbed Yamin's visit to the cloud fields of the north.

The cold winds were brisk under his gossamer yoke thei wings as he tumbled and laughed with his brethren high above the cloud-shrouded mountains. Here in the clear air where he could almost see the stars in midday, there were many yoke thei—the many facets of the spirit of the Yamani tree allowed free to play. There was the largest one—the Celestial King, the Thagyar Min, who foretold the fortunes of the coming year—and there was Min, the King, who represented the earthly Burmese king, who now remained in the cloud fields after his puppet effigy was shattered. These two important personages were conversing; and there were the prince and princess, Mintha and Minthamee, as usual dancing round and round and expressing their love. It would be fun to see a lover's spat now and then, but the best of Yamin's efforts had not brought such results.

At times, even with the wind in his wings in these high places and performing loops and dives to disturb the golden-headed geese formations as they winged north or south, he was bored, bored, bored.

This play that had always been his favorite thing seemed to have lost its flavor. It didn't demand his attention. It didn't make him really look and *see*. It didn't demand that he use his mind—not like a mystery.

A mystery was fun.

A mystery really was a most marvelous thing— even if it was dangerous and scary and sometimes deadly for a human.

Then something more than the brisk north wind streamed over his skin. Far away in the plains of Burma's south, his body moved. A warm wind graced his wood. Then rough, unknown hands held him.

Yamin stiffened. *What was happening?*

The hands let his wood fall.

All around him the winds were full of small bells jangling, the yoke thei disturbed in their play. Yamin turned, forgetting the others, and swooped south towards his body. It was a mystery, surely, for no one was allowed to touch the yoke thei except for their puppeteers and troupemates.

From behind came a cacophony of wild bells, his own chiming madly as his gossamer wings folded and he dove the long distance down the river, down over the cities of kings and the rice fields. Down over a vast plain that looked like a cactus, its dark spires and temples were so numerous. Once, he recalled, they had glittered in the sun.

And then he dove into his body, askew in his basket. The mud scent of unknown humans lingered on the air. Where was his puppeteer? Where was the troupe? Where was his old friend, the singer? He lay there wide-eyed and listening, for this was the worst kind of mystery—a nightmare, really. There the discordant ring of the gong circle as someone brushed against it. There a deep thump of a drum. And then there was a shout, a wicker crash, the sound of hooves, and more shouts.

Frowning, he scrambled to his knees, for surely an investigator such as him should learn what was happening. He pushed up the lid the smallest of amounts and peeked out. A small cook fire sputtered and smoked, almost out, when usually the musicians tended the flame to make rice. Beyond it stood a horse surely as large as an elephant cropping grass amidst scattered bamboo poles that were used for the stage. The usually neatly stacked puppet baskets had been pulled down. Baskets lay with their lids off, baskets on their sides. The mighty dragon drum had collapsed on top of the gong circle, and upended baskets of clothing were strewn over the drum circle.

Yamin sank back down in his basket in disbelief.

But what had happened? Something disastrous, surely. At least he *hoped* his puppeteers would not purposely leave their belongings like this. The alchemist puppet in his red robes lay in a tangle in the dust. The delicate foot of the princess's handmaiden poked out from under an upended basket. The golden tail of the naga serpent twitched above the edge of his open basket.

Yamin held in his shocked squeak with his hand. The yoke thei should never be treated like this. The alchemist was going to be *very* unhappy. He was a most particular puppet about his person. In fact, Yamin liked to play small jokes that would foil the little alchemist's perfect appearance.

Well, this would certainly do *that!* The dust alone would make the alchemist squeak. Yamin grinned and then remembered to be concerned and affronted. This was his troupe. Where were the humans?

Then two struggling men came into view. One, by the torn hem of his paso and the tangled twist of his turban, was a ruffian, but the other...!

Yamin sat up straighter and bumped his head on the basket top.

The man was big. A giant, surely. With hair the color of dusty rice, and clothed in a dusty jacket and two tubes that held his legs. They fought over something small and glittering.

Minthamee! The princess puppet, her creamy longyi and blouse covered in jewels. The small jeweled pins fell out of her hair and her hair fell loose in a raven cascade of softness. They could rip out her hair! They could break her limbs!

He went to shove open his basket to help her, but the small ruffian gave up and bolted out of the mess of baskets. The giant man straightened Minthamee's longyi and stroked her hair—a total affront, even if the gesture was gentle. He murmured something Yamin didn't understand.

Then a familiar shout came from a direction he couldn't see. The master puppeteer, the one called Saya Lin, for Yamin had begun to learn that humans had more than titles. The puppeteers came running, and the dust-haired giant turned and ran for his horse, Minthamee still in his hands.

Yamin leapt up to yell encouragement to the troupe, but they caught the strange giant without his help and dragged the hapless being back to the tangle of boxes. Yamin crouched down so that he wouldn't be seen, but could still watch the proceedings. The giant, for he stood at least a head above the master puppeteer, struggled in the arms of the puppeteers and Yamin's young apprentice puppeteer. The youngster was quite strong—for an apprentice. Something to be proud of.

Saya Lin examined precious Minthamee and passed her to her puppeteer for proper care, just as Yamin's old friend the singer puffed into view.

"What has happened?" the singer asked. He was old as human's judged age, with thin gray hair tucked up into a neat blue turban and he wore a long white shirt and paso tucked up to reveal spindly old man's legs. Thankfully, he no longer talked of retiring.

Well, Yamin could tell him, but instead the humans told half truths about how this man destroyed the camp.

Of course *he* could tell them what really happened, but since when had the puppeteers listened to him?

Except the old singer. He really was a decent human—even if he wasn't particularly good at finding them a mystery.

Then another puppeteer came into view carrying the small robed body of a boy.

It was too still to be alive.

Yamin looked back at the old singer. Perhaps his judgment had been too hasty.

§

Breathless and panting, Aung stood aghast at the edge of the wreckage of the troupe's noontime camp. His legs trembled and he swayed until Thura caught his arm.

"What has happened?" he panted.

The overturned wicker trunks and the tall man held prisoner by young Zeya, handsome Nai Zaya, and Nyein, the dragon drummer, gave him some idea. Saya Lin was worriedly uprighting the puppet baskets and examining their occupants.

His eyes widened at the height of the prisoner— taller than any Burmese, that was a certainty. He had faded brown hair—faded almost white at the forelock— and foreign, blue eyes, entirely too round at the corners that seemed unable to hide emotions. Right now, they were angry—and—indignant?

He wore dusty brown trousers that were worn black at the knees and a white shirt that had long ago traded its whiteness for gray, stained pink with dust. A light brown jacket hung open over his hips and he wore high black boots. Altogether too many clothes in this heat. The man's shirt was sodden with sweat and the reek of him made Aung pity his poor captors.

"What has happened?" he repeated.

"We found him going through the puppet trunks. He had Minthamee in his hands and ran for his horse when he saw us coming," Saya Lin said, looking up from his precious Thagyar Min.

Beyond the camp, amidst a tangle of bamboo poles, a saddled and bridled gray horse had dropped its head to graze. Its legs were longer than any horse he had seen this deep in Burma, though in the far south he had heard that foreigners were bringing in such creatures. Behind its saddle were stout leather packs that bristled with unknown equipment.

"A thief, then," Aung said. He looked at the disarray in what had been an orderly stacking of trunks. He stepped up to the foreigner and sought for the words. In their travels to the south he'd mostly ignored the foreigners, but when Thura had shown an interest in them, Aung had made a point of learning as much as he could about the English, including a little of the language. Saya Lin and he had practiced together, of like mind in thinking it was prudent to know how to deal with foreigners.

"What were you doing?" he asked and motioned at the disarray and the Minthamee puppet being carefully groomed prior to replacing her back in her trunk, even though she was still in her wood. The vain little princess would be most upset at being handled by a stranger—not even a Burman.

The man's round eyes widened—or Aung thought they did. It was sometimes difficult to read the foreigners' expressions given everything they felt competed so openly on their features. Far easier to read the Burman face that exposed only its deeper, uncontrollable emotions.

"You speak English! Thank God! There were two rascals searching through the trunks when I came riding by. I stopped them, but when no one came to claim the baskets, I thought I would examine them more closely. When your men came at me, I ran." He shrugged.

Aung studied his face, uncertain of all the words and whether the man's words were truth or a lie. The ground was scuffed by too many feet to be able to tell whether he told the truth.

"And where did they go?" he asked carefully, for it was some time since he had practiced regularly.

The man, his arms restrained, lifted his chin toward the fields south between their camp and the pahto.

"He's lying," Saya Lin said. "There was no one here but him when we arrived. There's no telling what we could have lost if we hadn't returned when we did."

Indeed, the foreigner's gaze kept slipping to Minthamee in the reverent hands of her puppeteer. The little princess' midnight hair was askew, some of the jeweled pins lost in her rough handling. Aung nodded Thura away to see if he could find them.

"Who are you? Why are you here?" Aung asked.

The man sighed and Aung realized that he was young, perhaps younger than middle age. There was something boyish about his face. Perhaps it was the bow of his mouth or the glint the sun placed in his strange blue eyes.

"My name is Harold Heath," he said in pidgin Burmese."I'm a surveyor from England." He stumbled over a word that sounded like "earth marker" to Aung. "The king sent me. I'm mapping your country."

Aung frowned. "Map?" And of more concern, "king." Surely Bodawpaya would not have hired such a man. He was loathe to have any involvement with the foreigners. His son, however...

Harold Heath tried to shrug loose of his captors, but they wouldn't release him. Finally, he used his foot to draw a line in the soil.

"Ayeyarwady." He drew a circle beside it. "Pagan." He drew another dot farther from the river. "Here."

"Map." Aung nodded tasting the foreign word that would be *myaypone* in Burmese. He was uncertain whether he liked the idea of foreigners creating a likeness of his country. He nodded at the packs behind the Harold Heath's saddle. "What?"

"Tools."

Aung left him and went to the horse. The creature was huge, its back taller than Aung's head and it swung a frightening, dark eye toward him. The creature huffed and stuck out its nose to sniff at Aung's chest. It snorted once and dropped its head back to the grass. Aung gingerly caught the horse's bridle and called Thura over.

"I will hold the horse and you empty the pouches."

Thura hesitated about nearing so large a beast but finally unbuckled the closure and pulled out a wooden pole in two pieces that cleverly fit together. Next was a carefully wrapped piece of metal filled with angles and curves. Aung looked his question at Harold Heath.

"A sextant. It is used to measure angles of the stars," he said in a wild mixture of barely comprehensible Burmese and English.

Like an astrologer? But what had that to do with maps?

There was a length of chain, and telescopes that could allow a man to see long distances—much to Thura's surprise when he turned one on the ornately carved corncob that topped the temple. He almost dropped the instrument. Then he brought out another carefully wrapped item, but what he recovered from the soft cloth was a carved Jataka stone like those Aung had seen on the temple walls.

Harold Heath was restive in his captors' hands.

Thura pulled out another bundle and unwrapped a finely carved alabaster reclining Buddha that someone had clearly chipped off of something larger. Thura placed the figure down and carefully bowed to it.

Aung turned to the foreigner. "I think you are a thief, Harold Heath. These are not things that would be freely given."

Harold Heath shook his head, his shock of lighter hair hanging over his eyes so that Aung could not read them—if it was possible to read such a man at all.

"I think...I think that this man may not be our friend," said Aung. "I think we should restrain him— perhaps tie him to a tree until we can decide what to do

with him. Besides, we have other matters to deal with."
He lifted his chin to U Myint, waiting patiently with
the small monk's body. "Where are those nuns? Surely
they must be finished their devotions by now."

Against his protests, Harold Heath was tied to
a htaung tree some distance away. His horse was left
to graze, once his pack of tools and stolen goods were
removed from the saddle. Inside there were more
carved statues and plaques. Even delicate, ancient
pieces of painted lacquerware wrapped in straw and
leather that had been taken from someone's household.
Harold Heath had been a busy man whatever he was.

He might indeed also be an "earth marker,"
for amongst his things were books filled with strange
scratchings that might be mathematical equations, and
rolled sheaves of paper with firm lines that wandered—
perhaps like a river—with small stars and more chicken
scratches beside them, and cross hatch small trees that
might indicate the landscape. The drawings were intricate
and beautiful as any inlaid carving on a lacquer bowl, and
yet it made Aung uncomfortable to see so vast and varied
a landscape represented in such a basic way. It was as if
Harold Heath saw the world around him in only lines and
blank spaces without seeing the people and the spirits
who inhabited the places. The stolen statues and plaques
emphasized that this was a man who saw the world as a
matter of reaping what he could for himself.

A living, hungry ghost always grasping for things and unable to let items or emotions go? For some reason Aung hoped not. The man was young; perhaps he had yet to learn the Buddhist lesson that all things pass away.

But then, he would not be Buddhist, would he?

From down amongst the trees, Harold Heath's oaths and pleas floated into camp. U Myint guarded the small monk's body as the others carefully checked their trunks.

And still there were no nuns.

Chapter 3

"He told the truth, you know."

Yamin poked his head up as he shoved off his basket lid and let it tumble to the ground. The old master singer swung around and looked cross for a moment—as if page puppets weren't supposed to express their opinions without being asked.

"Yamin! What are you doing? You could be seen!" The aging singer glanced in the direction of the tethered giant before crossing to him. Yamin put aside his irritation and surveyed the damage. It really was a most distressing scene with all the baskets and trunks awry, but mostly with poor Minthamee in such disarray.

"Is—is she all right?" he asked and tried to stop his lip from quivering. He might tease the princess, but it was only because he liked her. What would he do if she was beyond help, like the Min? What would they all do? His chest felt full and his vision momentarily blurred.

The singer checked over his shoulder and Yamin followed his gaze. His trunk was clearly screened from the giant by trees.

"It appears she is unbroken, though her clothing and jewels are torn and scattered," the singer said. He bent down to look Yamin eye-to-eye. "You truly are concerned, aren't you, little one? And perhaps a little scared. What did you see?"

The old singer settled himself on a trunk that carried equipment and Yamin leapt down from his trunk and settled beside him after checking once more that the giant couldn't see. Above them, the afternoon was waning. The doves coo-cooed in the trees and the cicadas hummed their high-pitched whine. What breeze there had been had died and the air seemed filled with dust that would surely get into all his joints and cause problems. He sighed and swung his feet back and forth.

"It really was most terrible. I was playing in the cloud fields of the north with the others. I swooped and dived and flew too close to the others so that the handmaid shrieked at me, but it was no fun at all. At least not as much as usual. In fact it had become rather boring, I think. But then I felt hands on my body that should not be touching me and I rushed back here." He nodded, thinking. "Everything was wrong, singer. There was no one here who should be! Just two ruffians and that man and his horse. They were fighting over Minthamee and then there was a shout and Saya Lin and the others got here. Just in time, I might add." He turned to the singer. "Where *were* they? We could have been killed! Minthamee could have been *stolen*!"

The singer bowed his head. "I am afraid it may have been my fault. There was a nun who collapsed by the temple. I called the troupe to help. In the quiet of the Pagan plain, I did not expect there would be bandits..." He sighed. "I suspect the others did not either. We know better now."

Yamin shook his head. It really was a travesty. The puppeteers were *supposed* to protect them!

The old singer turned to glance at the puppeteer who had once danced the garuda, before the garuda puppet disappeared. The troupe had been forced to accept that the garuda was most likely dead, and yet he had not appeared in the cloud fields of the north. Now that Yamin thought of it, that fact was truly strange. But the old singer wasn't motioning at the puppeteer as the reason, no, it was the thing he stood over. The body.

Right. In his worry for Minthamee, he'd forgotten about the mystery.

"He *is* dead, isn't he?" Yamin asked doubtfully.

The old singer nodded sadly. "And we do not know who killed him, or even who he is. The nun led us to the body and apparently we all trooped after her like fools and left our most important brethren unprotected. I cannot believe we did that. It is as if the world has gone askew and we with it." Since the bargain with the king of nats, Min Mahagiri, the old man had changed. He'd become even more thoughtful and less likely to do or say anything hastily, which at times was very trying. "There were two nuns who found him and requested our help. The nuns were supposed to join us here, but they have not come." The furrow of lines between the singer's gray-white brows said he doubted that they would ever arrive.

"Did they kill him, then? He looks very young." Yamin jumped down off the trunk and started toward the body U Myint still guarded, but caution stopped him. He did not want the giant to see him. The child—even from this distance he could see this was a human child—had tanned skin and the callused feet of someone who had spent his young life running barefoot—probably across these dusty plains—and playing in the river shallows. Yamin had noticed the shallows on their journey to Mount Popa because the troupe had found a quiet spot to have their lunch and Yamin had had the chance to dabble his toes in the water. It had been fun splashing the puppeteers until Master-no-fun, the old puppeteer that humans called Saya Lin, had threatened to douse him.

Yamin looked up at the old singer, thankful that he, at least, had never threatened him. "He's younger than my puppeteer."

The old singer nodded. "He is far younger. Zeya is seventeen. This boy looks perhaps ten. Too young to be dead, but someone has strangled him."

Yamin craned to see the boy's neck and took a step closer. There were deep blue bruises in a ring about his throat. The breeze brought a scent of incense and betel and something else he couldn't quite place.

"Here, now, have a care, Master Page. A dead monk is nothing for a puppet to trouble himself with," said U Myint, shooing Yamin back toward his perch.

Yamin stuck out his tongue and then scooted back to the protection of the old singer when the puppeteer threatened to come after him.

"*He* doesn't understand what it takes to solve a mystery," he said and plopped cross-legged onto the ground and trailed a finger in the red earth. "So who do you think killed him? Was it the giant or the men he chased away?"

The old singer turned his gray head to Yamin. Where previously the singer had seemed frail and like his bones tried to push free of his flesh, now flesh had begun to fill the hollows of his face and the bones of his knees no longer seemed to poke right through his paso.

"So you truly saw them fighting? You are certain it was not simply two fiends arguing over their spoils?"

Yamin thought a moment and nodded. "It was quite the battle. They said nothing to each other—just grunted and swore. Friends who were now enemies would surely say more. I think the giant spoke the truth—if you can believe a giant. I, myself, am not so sure, but then we can't very well leave him tied up to starve, either, can we? Buddha would not approve."

He frowned and found the singer smiling down at him.

"What? What is it?"

The old man shook his head. "You will forever surprise me, Yamin. Buddha, now. Who taught you of Buddha's lessons?"

Yamin tried to remember a lesson, but truly, in his long life no one had ever made him sit and learn.

"I think—I think I have just heard his lessons spoken many times. There were puppeteers and singers for this troupe even before you, you know. Perhaps it was when I was very young…" He scratched the base of one of his ponytails and wondered why, if his history was so long, he rarely thought of earlier times.

"So who are our suspects in the murder?" Yamin asked. "The giant? The ruffians?"

"A place to start," the old singer said. "But we may not investigate. Min Mahagiri said we should go to Yangoon, and Saya Lin wants to get that journey over with. Finding the young monk's killer may fall to others."

The master puppeteer came up to them from his inspection of the puppets. He glanced at Yamin, but then turned to the singer. "So? Where are these nuns of yours? I thought they were coming."

The singer shuffled to his feet and looked to the dark pile of the temple. Indeed it was an unpleasant enough looking place. Yamin wondered why anyone would build such a thing. Dark and chill and unpleasant, as if you were being swallowed up by the earth. He, for one, was smart enough not to go wandering inside such a place like the young monk had done. No wonder he'd ended up dead.

"Perhaps I should go back for them," the singer said.

"On your old legs?" the master puppeteer said. "We'll be waiting until tomorrow and I want to reach

Pagan town by nightfall. U Myint, go find them and bring them back. We'll have everything ready to leave when you return. Don't be long."

U Myint nodded and hurried down the footpath that looked like an unrolled lizard tongue snapping up those unwary enough to venture along its length. Yamin shivered and looked back at the singer. "What about the nuns? Could they have killed him?"

Both the master puppeteer and the master singer shook their heads.

"Why would they have called for us if they had killed him?" the singer said.

"Do not—I repeat, *do not*—drag us into investigating something that is not our business," said the master puppeteer, rudely shaking a finger at them. "We have had trouble enough these past six months. Understand?"

"Surely there is no harm in examining the evidence until we give the boy's body to his monastery," the singer said.

The master puppeteer's gaze narrowed. "Don't think I don't see what you're doing. You'll start an investigation, and by the time it's time to let the authorities investigate, you'll be convinced that you're the only one to solve the crime."

The old singer held up his hands. "Truly, I will hand it off. I'm weary of suspecting everyone. To prove it I will share Yamin's news. He saw the battle. It was as the foreign man said—he stopped ruffians from stealing the puppets. We should never have left them unattended."

"He had Minthamee in his hands," the master puppeteer said, shaking his head. "He was going to take her, just as he stole those things in his bags."

"We don't know that he stole them. He could have purchased them from someone local. Even if he did, do we leave him here, tied?" The singer shook his head. "Let him go. We will keep the stolen things and return them to the monks and the chief of the town. Then we can carry on to Yangoon. I do not like leaving him here. What if the authorities forget to collect him? He could die out here so far from anywhere."

That was it, Yamin realized. The old singer was still pained by how his words had led to a death in their last mystery. He could not stand the thought that someone else might die because of him. Yamin edged closer to his friend, reached up, and caught the singer's much larger hand.

"He is right, Master Puppeteer," Yamin said, throwing back his shoulders to look as imposing as sixteen inches could look. "He did not actually steal anything from you, though he might have taken things from a temple. Besides, setting him free might be good for your karma," Yamin added innocently.

If his knowledge of Buddha had surprised the old singer, there was no telling what knowledge of the wheel of dharma might do to another of the troupe. He'd begun to realize that the humans underestimated the yoke thei just as much as the yoke thei underestimated them. Very interesting, indeed.

The master puppeteer's eyes widened, but then he threw up his hands. "Fine. He shall go free, but first all our small charges must be safely in their baskets. Even you, Master Page." He harrumphed and stalked away.

Yamin watched him go and shook his head. "I really think he has even less sense of humor than you, singer." He looked up at the old singer and grinned.

§

The sky dimmed as the afternoon progressed. Clouds scuttled north from the Andaman coast, enveloping the blue sky. They cooled the air, but the day hung sullen and still around them as the afternoon faded away. By the moist scent of the occasional gusts of wind, dusk would bring rain. It was already raining eastward where they had come from. The streams of Mount Popa would be singing with new water and the

Taw Saun—the spirit of the mountain forest—would be happy.

Aung sat with the other puppeteers amidst the troupe's carefully repacked baskets and supply packs awaiting U Myint's return. The foreigner, Harold Heath, had been freed from his tether amidst the trees once the yoke thei were once more carefully hidden, but he had been kept from his horse and was under guard until the puppet troupe reached town. Saya Lin, ever suspicious, was still afraid that the foreigner and the ruffians were in league. He did not want the man calling compatriots down on the troupe while they were on the desolate roads of the ruins of Pagan.

Movement at the large central door of the temple brought Aung to his feet. His knees creaked, but he was no longer plagued by the old pain he'd suffered the past few years. Even with the weather changing, his gnarled fingers seemed less painful and there were times since his bargain with Min Mahagiri that he even thought some of his worn-out teeth chewed better. The little things that no one but an old man could appreciate.

U Myint came hurrying from the door of the temple, a trail of red dust rising into the air as he jogged down the path to the troupe. He was shaking his head as he arrived. "I've been around all four sides of all three levels of that infernal place. There's flowers and incense at every statue but no sign of any nun.

The damned women absconded without us. No telling where they'd be now."

"And we've wasted an entire afternoon waiting," Saya Lin said. "Enough. We'll carry the body into town and let them take care of it."

He motioned the troupe to their feet and they set off down the road, Aung relegated to leading the monstrous horse at the rear, for Saya Lin did not trust the beast's owner to lead it. There was also the chance that the stranger might be the murderer. He had been in the vicinity of the temple.

Even with the growing cloud bank, the air was hot. Whatever wind had shoved the clouds northward had done its job and then died so the air was sullen and stained with the scent of rain, river mud, and dust. Dust everywhere. Up Aung's nose and in his eyes, given the troupe preceded him down the road, their feet lifting the dust from the earth. The leather reins grew slippery in his hands and sweat dripped into his eyes off his old man's bushy brows. Red stained his shirt front.

Beside him the horse clopped quietly along and behind came U Myint carrying his small, umber-clothed burden, for Saya Lin did not trust the horse to carry the body.

The sun had fallen by the time they passed though the scrub-grass fields of small brick stupa, some still standing, many collapsed to a red brick heap on the ground. The cicadas' humming had reached a crescendo before the night insects took up the song and the bats fluttered and swooped through the twilight sky. Somewhere a neem tree bloomed for its perfume reached him, but then they reached a road where oxen wagons creaked and groaned on their way home and people walked at the side of the road.

Saya Lin turned them northward, down an avenue of broad trees and ancient, soaring temples. Candles lit their doorways, and from the west came the rushing hush of the great river.

Pagan town grew up around the road they followed, with walled households and the curved peaks of teak houses poking over the tops of the stone and mud walls that surrounded the household courtyards. Flowering bougainvillea covered the walls and the scent of cook fires sent Aung's stomach growling. Saya Lin would find a place for them to rest soon. The trouble was, they needed to find someone in authority to hand over both the horseman and the poor young monk's body.

Finally, Saya Lin stopped them beside a spreading tree where a woman was putting away her tea shop. The fire had been banked, the large kettle packed away, and a large, round-bottomed pot of oil covered with a cloth against the morning when she would once more make deep-fried rice dough for people to enjoy with their tea.

On a platform built chest-high on the tree sat a coconut, a small pile of rice, a bunch of small ripe bananas, and a mango. A garland of marigolds hung from the small platform. It was an offering to both the tree spirit and to Min Mahagiri. Aung bowed to the coconut, the villagers' effigy of Min Mahagiri, and exhaled a little of his worry, for the nats were still honored openly here. It was a good sign—regardless of the wreckage of the nat images at the first temple.

"Excuse us," Saya Lin interrupted the woman's labors and bowed. "We are a royal puppet troupe traveling from Mount Popa to Yangoon. We have come across a body and would report it to the village headman. Where can we find him?"

The woman once had been a black-haired beauty, but now age had broadened her middle and creased her face with smile lines. She eased her back as she looked them over. Then her gaze reached the foreigner and the burden U Myint carried. Her gaze widened with concern. "Who? What child is this?"

She abandoned her kettles and pots and went to the body to gaze into the small face. Her hand came to her mouth and then she sighed. "It is Khun Khine's boy, strangled." She looked sharply at Aung. "Where did this happen?"

"He was found in Dhammayangyi temple," Aung said.

Her mouth firmed into a hard line that revealed hints of old grief. Finally, she nodded. "His family farms north of the village though it is a poor living. The boy entered the monastery this past fall. His parents were so proud."

Her gaze swung back to Saya Lin, but Aung could tell there was something she wasn't saying. "What happened? Was he alone?"

"Those are things we must tell the authorities first," Aung said, stopping Saya Lin's reply with a raised hand.

She nodded and wiped her hands on a cloth, then straightened her longyi around her hips. "I will take you."

She led off, taking them down dusk-filled streets between walled compounds until they reached a gate beyond which a two-story teak house loomed in the growing darkness. She knocked on the gate. "Nai Naing! Answer your gate. There is urgent business!"

The puppeteers had set down their burdens. It was long they had walked and longer still since they had eaten. The musicians cast themselves down on the ground just as someone opened the gate.

A portly, bald man stood there, fighting to keep his loosely-wrapped turban on that smooth pate. "What do you want, Htet Hla? Surely there is nothing that can't wait until morning."

Then he caught sight of the crowd beyond Htet and he frowned. "What is this? Who are these people?"

"A royal puppet troupe—the royal troupe from Popa," Htet Hla said as if she took some pleasure in announcing their presence.

Aung cringed, for this could only mean that their reputation had preceded them here, too. Did Saya Lin realize what this could mean?

Nai Naing stepped through his gate to Saya Lin. "Well met. Well met, indeed. It is a pleasure to meet those who brought a killer to justice!" He bowed, his hands palms-together at his forehead. "You have done us great service."

Saya Lin cast an unhappy glance at Aung before bowing in return, his hands at face height. "I thank you for your welcome. We have a problem. We stopped to rest near one of the great pahtos on the road to Pagan town and were called into the temple by two nuns. They had found a body inside."

Saya Lin motioned for the troupe to let U Myint through and the steadfast puppeteer carried his burden forward to gently lay the young monk on the earth before Nai Naing.

"It is Khun Khine's boy," said Htet Hla. "I recognize him."

Nai Naing stepped back and frowned. "Why bring him here? He should be with his family or his monastery!"

He looked as if he wished to escape back through his gate and close it against them.

Aung stepped forward. "Someone in authority must assume the investigation," he said.

"But...but...surely that is you!" Nai Naing said. "There is no one in Pagan town with such a skill. We are farmers and merchants and fishermen."

"There are suspects and witnesses," Aung tried again. "This man was near the scene." He motioned to Harold Heath. "There were ruffians seen and then there were the nuns who called us, but disappeared instead of returning to lead us into town. Someone must find them and question them."

Nai Naing held up his hands as if to ward off Aung's words. "There! See! You know what to do! You found the body, you must solve this thing!"

"But what of the boy's body? Surely it must be sent to family or monastery?"

Nai Naing looked from the small corpse to Htet Hla. "Deal with it as you see fit."

Then he ducked back into his courtyard, slamming the gate behind him.

Aung turned from the closed gate to Saya Lin's glare and sighed.

He had not planned it to be this way, but he doubted Saya Lin would believe him, and each time the troupe was drawn into an investigation he felt his old friend grow more distant from him. This turn of events had widened that gulf to near as wide as the Ayeyarwady.

Chapter 4

The basket bounced with the slow steady tread of Zeya's feet as he carried Yamin to wherever they were going. Usually Yamin slept when the troupe was moving, but this time the excitement of another mystery to solve had made returning to the cloud fields of the north rather unappealing. His chest was almost bursting with excitement.

Yamin waited as long as he could bear before he pushed up the lid of his basket the tiniest bit to see. Cooler night air burdened with the scent of muddy water flooded into the basket. The river. He had smelled the great Ayeyarwady River at its birthplace high in the mountains. Here its clear scent of snow had become murky and filled with the deep notes of pools of dark water and the fishy scent of river horses. Beside his basket, the young singer walked with his burden of bamboo stage poles bristling on his back. Behind him came the old singer, leading the giant's horse.

This journey had gone on far longer than Yamin had expected. That the troupe had brought the foreigner with them did not bode well for Yamin's freedom.

He slumped back into his basket, plotting how he would get around that particular problem, just as the voices of Saya Lin and a woman rose and his basket was set down with a thump and a great heaved sigh from his puppeteer. Yamin bit back an oath at the jarring fall. He was definitely going to have a talk with his young apprentice puppeteer.

Around the basket arose the hubbub of setting up camp. He tipped the lid up again and peered out into darkness and the scent of water. The river was very close, for the sound of rushing water was like the wind through branches and the air was too damp. If they stayed here, his pantaloons and vest would soon enough be cold and clammy. Minthamee would not be pleased. He could imagine her sweet voice complaining to her puppeteer, and when Minthamee was unhappy—well, everyone had to know about it.

The musicians had started a small cook fire and its meager light reflected off the tall brick stupa that sprang up through tall grass like potent weeds. The puppeteers were busy making camp, and to one side, the master puppeteer and the old master singer were talking intently to a woman Yamin didn't know. Then there was much bowing and the woman left them, disappearing into the darkness. Now would be a good time to seek out the old singer, but at the edge of the firelight the glow caught on the pale head of the giant and his horse—now unsaddled. The gray coat of the horse picked up the glimmer of moonlight as the moon rose over the horizon.

Well, this was a pretty predicament. Just how did the old singer expect him to investigate when a foreigner—someone who definitely should not know about the yoke thei—was sitting right in camp?

Yamin frowned. If the old singer thought this could confine him to his basket, he had another thought coming.

Lifting the basket lid a little higher, Yamin considered the light and shadows of the camp. Thankfully there were more shadows, something that worked to his advantage. The baskets were set in a cluster at one side of the camp, and it looked like sleeping mats had been spread around them. Well, at least the humans were trying to protect them, for once.

He inched up the basket a little higher and swung a leg over the side, then slipped-slid out of the basket to the ground. That was better. It was always nice to feel the earth between his toes.

The trouble was, without the height of his basket stacked on top of the naga's basket, it was difficult to see where everything was. He scuttled through the shadows, keeping the baskets as a barrier between himself and the troupe, until he neared the place where he thought he'd last seen the old singer. He slipped between the baskets to the space around the fire.

Success! While the other troupe members lounged on the ground, the old singer sat on a three-legged stool with his back toward Yamin. Yamin crept up behind him and tugged at his paso.

The old singer didn't respond.

Yamin tapped his toes a moment, before reaching up and catching hold of an old fleshy butt-cheek and pinching.

As he leapt to his feet, the old singer almost pulled Yamin off the ground. The old man spun around. "You!"

Quick as a wink he grabbed Yamin up and left the firelit circle.

"What do you think you're doing, Yamin? Can't you see how dangerous it is? There's a foreigner in our camp who thinks it is fine for him to touch a royal puppet!"

Yamin struggled in his grasp until finally he sat up in the old man's arms with his hands on his hips. "Now you listen to me! There is a mystery and I am most determined to be involved in the investigation. I will not be kept like baggage!"

"Shh!" the old singer looked over his shoulder.

Yamin followed his gaze. "You see? The giant is still beside his horse. There is no problem."

The old man brought his face close to Yamin. "You listen to me, Master Page. Your voice carries. You must learn to whisper and to be very careful—do you understand? I do not wish to exclude you, but there are many people about and we don't know any of them or if they were involved in the murder."

Yamin perked up. "So we're going to investigate?"

Shaking his head, the old singer settled Yamin on the ground and knelt beside him. "I don't know. We've been asked to, but Saya Lin resists. And the woman tells us that the headman is a vindictive sort— that if we fail to investigate there is just as much chance the headman will claim that we are responsible for the young monk's death. We were just deciding what to do when your presence forced me to leave the discussion."

Yamin gave him his best innocent face. "I was only intent on helping."

The roll of the old man's eyes said he doubted the truth of the statement and Yamin scratched the base of one of the two ponytails crowning his head.

"They couldn't possibly decide to leave, could they? I mean, leave a mystery unsolved? How could they? I, myself, could never do such a thing."

Another roll of the old singer's eyes and Yamin kicked him in his thigh. "The least you can do is pretend that you want my help. You've become entirely less fun since Min Mahagiri took away some of your age. Perhaps there is merit in growing old—you gain a better perspective on things. Take me, for example. I am very old."

"You scamp!" The old man's smile was the affectionate one Yamin favored. "Of course we will investigate together. But you must be very careful. More careful than ever you have been. I have seen this kind of foreign man before, and unlike a villager who will back away from a rustle in the bushes for fear of angering a spirit, this one will investigate if only to prove whether it was only the wind. Do you understand?"

Yamin thought a moment. "You mean he is curious?"

The singer nodded. "About everything. His kind—it is not only the need to understand—they need to possess everything. What better item to possess than a spirit-inhabited page?"

Yamin stumbled back a pace, his small heart thumping. "Me? He would want to possess me?"

"He might."

Yamin went up on tiptoe to peek around the baskets and across the fire to where the giant sat. The man's hands were so large, surely they could swallow him up. Certainly, they could break him apart. Solemnly he turned back to the singer and nodded. "I will be very careful."

§

Maybe, just maybe, the little puppet had understood the graveness of their situation. Maybe, just maybe, the small, troublesome page would remember long enough to be cautious.

Maybe.

Aung looked in the direction of the little page's basket where Yamin had faded away into the shadows and darkness. The trouble was, the little page meant well, and truly he *had* been of aid in their last two investigations, but this time things were entirely too dangerous for a puppet. Even a spirit-inhabited one.

He went back into the circle where the discussion had flagged. Thura looked up at him and nodded.

"We stay—for now," he murmured. "The others took your side against Saya Lin. He is not happy."

Aung followed his apprentice's gaze across the fire to where Saya Lin's frozen features betrayed his anger. He glanced at Aung and nodded. "It seems you have your way, Singer. You have five days to solve this thing."

It was unheard of, that a troupe would go against the decision of their leader and manager, but Saya Lin was not a true manager and was only their leader by default since they had lost their previous manager in Amarapura. Apparently Saya Lin's undefined status left the troupe more comfortable following their own opinions.

"So what do we do now, Aung?" U Myint asked.

"Yes. How do we proceed with our investigation?" Yamin's young puppeteer, Zeya, asked.

The twenty others of the troupe, musicians and puppeteers alike, were nodding and all of them looked as if they were ready to run off into the dark to do whatever he said for the investigation.

He looked at each one and back to Saya Lin. "I thank you for your offer of assistance, but our first task is to keep our small charges safe. I suggest that in addition to guarding our guest, we spend this night in contemplation of what we know and what we need to learn."

The others looked disappointed, but soon left the fire to settle on the bamboo mats around their baskets, while Nyein, the dragon drummer, went to guard Harold Heath. The foreigner had also bedded down beside his own small fire apparently content to stay with them until the matter was sorted out and his belongings returned to him. His horse had wandered from the firelight, but his gray coat became a misty form in the dark, with the click of a hoof on a rock and the sound of torn grass and chewing comfortable signs that all was well.

Aung stood from his stool and felt the slight twinge in his knees.

He needed to think, and often, going for a walk cleared his head. It was odd, but sometimes it seemed as if the answers he needed simply hung in the air awaiting to be found. Hands behind his back, he started across the brick-strewn field, through the deep grass toward the river.

Between steep gravel and mud banks, the Ayeyarwady River ran wide here, so wide the far side of the channel was a distant shadow against the silver of the moonlit river waves—when the moon poked its nose through the clouds. The clouds were moving again, jostling through the heavens as the wind streamed them northward. There would be rain in the great mountains that ranged across that part of the world. Some might even give up their moisture on Amarapura, but standing on the edge of the parched Pagan plain, it was hard to believe it might fall here.

During the day the river would be busy with small, plaid-sailed fishing boats and booms of teak logs traveling southward to the shipbuilders of Yangoon. Along the shore, women would wash their bright laundry and spread it to dry. Children would play, their laughter ringing over the water. But now it was quiet, with just the wind in the grass and the rush of the water.

Peaceful. So hard to believe that in a supposedly peaceful place like the old temple, something evil had befallen the young monk whose body was now either in the hands of the monks or his family—Htet Hla had assumed responsibility for the arrangements. But Aung had begun to realize that there was the possibility of evil wherever there were humans. Which meant that the list of possible suspects in the murder were impossibly broad.

A rustle in the grass beside him stopped his contemplation.

"I hear you, Yamin. Show yourself. You're not as stealthy as you think."

The grass rustled again and then Yamin leapt out.

"Ta da!" he said, arms spread wide for approval as he landed before Aung. "You didn't know that I was following you, did you?"

He nodded, though in truth he had suspected that it would be the case. Yamin had begun to remind Aung of a dog worrying a precious bone whenever a mystery presented itself. The page just wouldn't let go.

"I am sitting here thinking of suspects, so perhaps you can add your thoughts," Aung said.

Yamin gave a forceful nod and settled himself at Aung's side.

"Well, there is the giant. He was around," Yamin offered.

"Yes. He was. Close enough that he could have killed the child and then climbed on his horse and ridden to our camp."

"He could have gotten there very quickly with that horse's long legs," Yamin said.

"True. And there were those ruffians you mentioned. Can you describe them for me?"

Yamin scratched the base of his ponytail and looked out into the darkness. "I didn't see them well because it happened so fast. There was the giant and I think I looked most at him. Very strange, that one—and so big. Did you see the size of his hands?" He shivered and cocked his head. "There was one man who simply ran. He had black hair and a plaid paso. The man who fought the giant—well, I think he might have been as tall as you. He wore a yellow turban—it was very dirty—and his paso was faded. I think it might have been torn along the hem, but he wore it like pantaloons so it is hard to say."

The little page turned a moon face to Aung. "Does that help?"

Aung smiled affectionately down at him. "Everything helps, my friend."

Yamin sighed and leaned in against him. "There are the nuns, of course. Why did they leave us with the corpse? Not very nice of them. I, myself, would not have done that." He looked up at Aung. "When you die, singer, I will not leave your side—ever."

"Very kind of you, Yamin. But you will have to, sometime. You see, they will want to either bury or burn my body. A body can't just be left lying around, you know."

"The young monk was..." Yamin said. "But I suppose the flies and the smell would be bad." He brightened and leaned forward to look out at the river. "Look! River horses!" He pointed.

Far out on the river, pale, sleek forms dolphined through the glimmering water. It was a good omen, for the magical river horses were known to aid drowning sailors and at the moment Aung felt like he was drowning in this case, for though they knew a few of the people who had been nearby when the body was found, truly anyone could have met the young monk in the temple and done him harm.

"I think—I think tomorrow we must learn more about this young monk and we need to know who was near the temple. Our giant friend may be able to help us with that."

Aung stood, happy that he had his course of action planned. With the troupe's assistance he should be able to gather information much more quickly and solve the matter within a day or two.

Yamin scrambled up beside him. "And we need to find those nuns."

"Of course we do." Aung nodded. It should be a simple matter. "How many of them can there be in a place like Pagan?

Chapter 5

The morning proved that there were far more nuns than Aung had supposed. Enquiries had discovered that there were a number of small communes of nuns scattered amongst the far-flung villages spread over the Pagan plain. Unlike their far more numerous monk brethren who sought alms every morning and whose great monasteries were supported by the people's giving, the nuns kept to small enclaves. They worked for a living, supporting themselves through their gardens, their weaving, and other skills.

Aung used the energy of the puppeteers and sent two of them out to enquire after the nuns. The troupe did, after all, have the women's names.

Aung watched the pair leave and turned back to the camp. The day was young, the sky blue. Surprisingly, it had not rained in the night and the clouds had been driven northward—perhaps to rain on mighty Amarapura. The troupe's breakfast of rice and fish purchased from a fisherman by the river was still fresh and warm in Aung's belly. They had shared their bounty with Harold Heath, who had settled himself back beside his own hearth. He seemed in no hurry to leave, which seemed odd, but then who was Aung to judge the motivations for a foreigner? Even Saya Lin seemed to have eased his need to keep the large man a prisoner.

The air was cool, the slanted sunlight bright and already warm as it nosed between the dark spires of the ancient stupa and temples. The sunlight caught on the tops of trees, and burnished wild flowers. The river hummed and in the distance could be heard the voices of the fishermen returning with their earliest catch of the day for Pagan market. Birds twittered in the trees. Butterflies bobbed above the grasses where the sunlight turned the dew caught on spider webs into ropes of jewels. It was a good place, where Saya Lin had led them. With his need for routine and order, the man was built to be a troupe leader, though he had no desire for the task. It was a shame that he carried the role like a burden instead of recognizing the skill he had. If he assumed the role fully and relinquished his puppeteer duties, the troupe would surely show him the deference the leadership inspired. There would be no more incidents like last night where Saya Lin's decision was overruled.

A Death in Passing

At the moment, Saya Lin was busy speaking with a villager who had joined them this morning. Thura was telling stories with the musicians. Yamin was—hopefully—still in his basket like a well-behaved yoke thei page. He smiled, thinking of the little one's level of frustration at being confined. Well, Yamin would have to remember about the dangers of being out and about when you are only sixteen inches tall—more so with a foreigner in their midst.

A foreigner who may have even seen the killer as he rode across the plain—if he was not the killer himself. There was no help for it. Aung would have to interview the man.

From his stool by the fire, for even with the nat's help he felt the chill and stiffness of morning, he stood and shuffled to the foreign man's camp. He nodded at the dragon drummer, who stood on guard nearby.

Harold Heath reclined on a blanket, his hands behind his head as he dozed. Beside him, open on the blanket, was the book Aung had seen in the man's saddle bags. The wind fluttered the pages before Aung could quite see the drawing the large man had made. It looked like it might have been of Minthamee. There were other drawings, too, of members of the puppet troupe—even one Aung recognized as himself.

Aung cleared his throat and the man's off-putting blue eyes flashed open.

"Why, hello." He sat up. "What can I do for you?"

The man stank, of course. It was as if the foreigner had never heard of washing and his stained white shirt proved it. Aung crouched upwind of him.

"I must ask you further questions about yesterday," Aung said, hesitating over the odd combination of simple Burmese and awkward English.

Harold Heath motioned to the earth beside him and Aung sank down, cross-legged.

"Thank you for your help," Harold Heath said haltingly. "I fear I would still be tied if not for you. So what do you plan to do with me?" He mimed being tied like a pig being trussed for market and they shared a smile.

"Do with you? If you did not kill the boy, there is nothing that we will do, but I appreciate you staying." And it supported the notion that the man was innocent—at least of the murder. "It appears that you study us," he said with a nod at the fluttering pages of the book."

Harold Heath colored slightly. "I record what interests me."

Aung bowed his head as he gathered his thoughts. Was it good that the puppet troupe interested this man? "Yesterday. Tell me what you saw as you neared the temple."

Harold Heath frowned. He shrugged. "There was nothing really. A lot of old temples. A lot of parched grass. There was a pile of wicker trunks by the entrance road to one of the large temples. Two men were going through them. I stopped them. They looked suspicious for there was no way two men could carry all of them. We got into a fight."

"Tell me about before you reached the temple." He raised his hand to stop Harold Heath's shake of his head. "What did you see? Think back. It is important."

Dutifully, the large foreign man closed his eyes in contemplation. His shock of lighter hair fell over his forehead. "I was coming from the south. I'd been visiting some of the smaller temples along the river with a friend who had gone his own way. I saw that behemoth temple and thought that I'd visit. You never know what you might see."

Aung recalled the contents of the man's saddle bags. Or steal, more likely. Perhaps the attempted theft of Minthamee was simply a crime of opportunity that had been caused by Aung's call for help. The troupe always responded to the call of one of their own. In future they would need to change that approach—regardless of who called for help. The countryside was changing and thieves were no longer hesitant to steal from performers under royal patronage.

"Dust had risen down the road to the temple, so someone had passed that way. I think—I think I might have seen dust rise behind the temple, too." He opened his eyes. "I'm sorry. That's all."

"No plowmen? No carts? No one walking down the road?"

"There was an oxcart. It carried a huge terra cotta urn. It must have been full given the way the wooden wheels groaned and the oxen strained. It was just south of the temple. There were two men."

Aung straightened. Two men. Usually those carts held only the driver.

"Can you describe the cart or the men?"

The big foreign man shrugged. "How can you expect me to remember?"

Taking a chance, Aung reached and snagged the man's book. He flipped it open to the writing and the images—a strikingly good image of the princess puppet considering how briefly the man had held her. The other images caught the thoughtfulness of U Myint's expression and the liveliness of Zeya. His own image gazed seriously back at him. He tapped the page. "These do. And you make notes as you travel to make your map—and perhaps other things. That tells me that you see what is around you. A seeing man does not forget—especially when murder is involved."

There. He had made it clear he would not accept this man's lazy recollections. Clearly, this man was an agent of foreign powers and as such he would record everything. Unless he was the murderer.

Harold Heath sighed. "One was a young man clad in only a breechclout. His hair was tied up on his head and a loose rag was tied around his head. I believe it was faded red. He appeared to be the driver of the cart. The other man wore one of those skirt-things like you and them." He raised his head at the village man and Saya Lin, still deep in conversation. "It was blue and looked almost new. His shirt—it was brown—looked clean and new, as well. He wore a turban carefully coiled on his head like a snake—nothing like the cunning twists of those Indian Pasha blokes."

He watched Aung as if awaiting his approval and for a moment Aung wondered whether he could trust this man's testimony. He decided to trust until trustworthiness was disproven.

Aung bowed his head. "Thank you. Is there anything else?"

Harold Heath shook his head. "Just a whole lot of questions. Like what are those dolls you're carrying? You lot guard them like they're your children. What are you?"

Aung inclined his head. "Our introduction was hasty. I am Aung of the royal puppet troupe. We are the yoke thei, the most ancient of puppet troupes, beloved by all and patronized by King Bodawpaya himself."

Harold Heath's gaze narrowed slightly. "So, you know the king, then. And those baubles on your puppets—they aren't just paste, are they?"

Paste. Aung tasted the word, not understanding.

"False," Harold Heath said. "A lie. Not a ruby. Not a pearl."

The question became clear. "They are real, as befitting the puppets. They are royalty as well." Aung said, careful of his words. Avarice shone in the man's blue gaze.

"Interesting," Harold Heath said. "I should like to see them again. They looked quite wonderfully made. A wonder of craftsmanship I should like to examine."

Aung's blood ran cold. This man bore careful watching, for there was something about him. The man carried secrets. Aung pushed up to standing and nearly fell. Even his revived legs were not what they once were.

"That is not possible. The yoke thei are not brought out unless there is a performance, and they are not examined by anyone other than their puppeteers."

Harold Heath looked up at him mildly. "More's the pity, isn't it?"He picked up the open book he'd apparently been reading and idly flipped the page. "I think perhaps I'll travel with you and learn."

Aung wasn't sure what to say. He nodded once more to the dragon drummer and returned to Saya Lin, coming up beside him as the village man hurried away from the camp.

"I fear you were right, old friend," Aung said. "It was not a good idea to stay here and it was a worse idea bringing the foreigner with us, though he may yet prove to be the killer."

Saya Lin glanced at him, but there was still a difference in his gaze. "What brings this on? I thought you liked it when things went your way. If you wish to be in charge, Aung, perhaps I should step back."

The warmth that had always been between then had diminished greatly and the gulf had widened.

"Not so." Aung shook his head. "Not so at all. I only try to do what is right."

"For you or for the troupe?"

Aung frowned. "Of course, for the troupe! At this moment, I come to speak to you about the troupe! We must guard the puppets well and perhaps we should leave immediately. I fear that man's interest in the yoke thei. He has already asked to touch them. I have told him that is not possible, but I would not put it past him to try to get to them again. I thought we could return his things and change our camp, but it seems he has decided to stay with us to learn about us—or so he says!"

Saya Lin went still. "Then I fear we have a problem. The villager that I met with is a merchant. His first child has just been born and he wishes to host a pwe to seek the spirits' blessing. He has commissioned us to perform—at a very handsome fee, I might add. Our purse could use the coin after the debacle at Popa—and Amarapura." He rocked on the balls of his feet, clearly pleased with himself.

It was clear from Saya Lin's expression that he would not change his mind and it would be hypocritical of Aung to try to change it—especially so if he wanted to support Saya Lin as troupe leader. Besides, it was true that their purse was almost empty. They had not waited for the king's full payment, but had taken their leave in fear of the king requesting yet another performance—this one with the king puppet that they no longer had. Performances such as this for the merchant were the key to the troupe's survival.

Aung bowed his head. "Then I pray you warn the troupe to be ever on their guard."

Saya Lin nodded. "We will tell them together, but I fear there may be a larger problem in a certain small one. He does not listen."

"Not to anyone, at all," Aung nodded. "I will speak to him, but he will not be happy—not with the mystery unsolved."

"So solve it," Saya Lin said. "Solve it so we can move on and not have to listen to you moaning about what we should have done."

The words struck Aung like a blow to the gut. When they had been simply Master Puppeteer and Master Singer, never had they shared a cross word. But then Saya Lin began to walk another path...

And now this. Loss filled Aung's chest. The wind gusted off the river as Saya Lin left him to speak to the troupe members still lounging around their morning meal. There were others Aung needed to talk to: the boy's family and the monastery he belonged to. Just how had the young monk come to be at a dark temple so far from Pagan village?

Leaving word with Thura regarding his errand, he set out through the grass toward the road.

"Psst."

It sounded like a cross between a snake and a bird. Aung checked, but spotted neither and kept going.

"Psst!" A little louder and a clump of grass rustled to his right.

Aung stopped and checked behind him. Beyond the trunks he could just make out Harold Heath apparently still engrossed in his book. He looked back to the clump of grass that had mysteriously grown eyes and two bobbing black ponytails amid the golden grass tassels.

"You should not be here, Yamin. You should not be out of your box!" Aung said as he scanned the nearest of the many brick stupa crumbling under the sun.

Yamin crept out of his clump of grass. "I knew you would say that, but I wanted you to know that I kept watch on the foreigner last night. When even the drummer was asleep, he circled the camp as if he was searching for a way into our trunks. I do not like him, Singer. When he looked at the trunks I saw hunger in his eyes."

Aung sighed and closed his eyes at the worry that constricted his chest. "I know. And I fear he does not tell the truth, either. But I cannot say to arrest him because he is the killer, and neither can I say he did not do it and send him away when he has decided to stay.

We have no evidence against him other than proximity to the temple and that he was seen holding Minthamee, who he claims he was protecting. I suppose that in some ways we are fortunate that he stays with us while we conduct our investigation. That fact alone suggests his innocence." Or that he wanted something—like Minthamee? "We cannot be seen to let the killer go free."

Yamin looked up at him crossly. "So where are you going then? Off to complete the investigation and leave me behind?"

What could he say? Finally, he nodded. "Not to complete the investigation, but to conduct it. I plan to speak to the family and to those at the young monk's monastery."

Yamin thought about it and nodded. "You want to know more about him and what could take him to that temple."

"Exactly. And it is not exactly possible for you to come along in broad daylight."

The little puppet frowned. "True enough." Then he brightened. "But I could pretend to be in my wood as I did at Popa. It was most successful there!"

Aung shook his head. "I don't think that is a good idea. I will go much farther today. Can you truly be so still for an entire day?"

"I, myself, can be incredibly still—if I want to be," Yamin said and puffed himself up, before standing absolutely immobile. Even his gaze was frozen. "Pick me up," he whispered with barely a lip move.

Aung looked to the heavens. Saya Lin would likely kill him for taking the page with him, but if he didn't take Yamin, there was a very good chance the little one would follow anyway—with a great more certainty that he would be found.

Against his better judgement, he picked Yamin up. Just what explanation he would have for even bringing the jolly puppet with him escaped him at the moment. He just needed to get on with it. He marched out of the temple-pocked field and turned north on the road. Pagan town was in this direction. The boy's family was this way and so was the monastery.

He just hoped that he wasn't also treading the path of disaster.

§

The old singer was actually quite an able bearer. He walked carefully over the rutted road, whether to protect his old bones or for his passenger's benefit, Yamin didn't know, but it was appreciated.

He twisted slightly in the singer's arms and the old singer hissed down at him.

"I just want to see better," he whispered from the side of his mouth. It was actually fun to try to speak without his lips moving.He was getting pretty good at it, if he did say so himself. Perhaps it was something Saya Lin would let them use in the show. Perhaps he could even sing his own songs! Now wouldn't that be fun! Of course, the young singer, Thura, who sang for him, was actually fairly good at capturing a sense of play. However, it was something to think about on another day.

Today there was just so much to see! Frankly, he didn't ever want to have to travel in his musty old wicker trunk again! It was no wonder the yoke thei went to the cloud fields, but if this was an alternative…

Old men and women gathered under a tree sipping tea. The thannaka paste on the women's cheeks caught in their wrinkles and made their faces caricatures of the fine maidens they had once been. Mothers pounded rice in the shadows of their stilted houses. Others worked looms, weaving their cloth. A man with a muddy paso hem walked past carrying a pole on which were strung clumps of young rice plants, so somewhere there was water enough to grow them. The road ahead split and a long line of oxcarts filled the road down to the river, the carts filled with the huge terra cotta urns waiting to be laboriously filled with river water, bucketful by bucketful. The oxen pairs strained to haul fully burdened carts up the slope from the river.

And there were children!

Yamin almost craned to see two youngsters chasing a wicker ball. They dashed across the road, kicking it with their feet. His toes itched to join them. He'd never had a ball to chase—something he must see to for the future. There really was so much that had been hidden from him all these years confined to a wicker box. Had it been done on purpose?

More children chased each other around the stilts of a house. Still others ran down the road, to where he couldn't see. Monks in russet-colored robes shuffled down the street with bowls in their hands, stopping at each household where the woman would place rice or money in the bowl.

The old singer turned off the main road toward a glistening temple with a tall, bell-shaped dome that had bits of mirror sunk into its white flanks. Monks scurried about, carrying the long rectangular lacquer panels that held Buddha's holy scriptures. There were others lounging on the low walls along the road and young monks playing. Even though they ran out of sight, he could hear their laughter.

The temple was built like most temples he'd seen, not that he'd seen many, of course. A broad flat platform provided a base for the domed stupa to rise from a square base up to a second platform that held a second layer square base, and then a third before rising up into the tall pointed dome that was topped with a three-layer lacy silver hti that was a ceremonial umbrella. Each of the platforms held many smaller spires that held niches that contained holy figures including those of the Great Nats. From his angle, some of the small, silver spires looked twisted and misshapen.

But the singer didn't go to the platform to make an offering. Instead he turned off on a secondary road that led to crumbling walls around a stilted teak monastery that stood on the river bank. Mango trees and papaya gave shade to groves of banana palms. Beside the main building, which had uplifted eaves above round windows and broad doors, stood lesser buildings that from the smoke rising must contain kitchens and perhaps dormitories. There were many monks here and an older man leaning on a cane approached them.

As with all monks, his head was shaved and he had the orange-stained lips and teeth of the betel nut chewer. He was clad in the same umber robes as other monks, but the cloth of his robes seemed fuller as if there was more wrapped around his body. He had a round face, but he could never be called jolly for small creases deeply marred his brow between his eyes and more lines painted a downward turn to his mouth—a lot like some of the puppet king's senior advisors. Those old fuddy-duddies never smiled!

The man bowed with his hands pressed together at his breast. The singer set Yamin down and it was sorely tempting to just run off, but he held to feigning he was in his wood as the old singer copied the old monk's bow.

"I am Master Nu," said the monk. "I am a teacher here. I believe you may be from the yoke thei troupe that arrived last night." The monk nodded down at Yamin and Yamin held himself especially still, for the old monk's eyes were black as if he *knew* things. Hopefully what he knew was not about the yoke thei.

"Correct." The old singer bowed again and retrieved Yamin as if he knew of his temptation. "We came into town bearing sadness, for we found the body of a young monk on our journey. I believe he may have been one of your novices. We are told he was the son of Khun Khine."

Master Nu's face grew pained as he closed his eyes and nodded. "Young Hlaing Htay is a novice here. Are you sure it is him that you found?"

The singer seemed to hesitate and Yamin wanted to frown. Surely the monastery had missed the young monk. Had they more than one who was missing?

"He was identified by a woman in the town. She had the body taken to the family."

"What! But he should have been brought here. While he is a novice, the Sangha—the monks—are his teachers and family!"

Aung bowed again. "I apologize, I thought we did the right thing. Can you tell me when Hlaing Htay was missed?"

Master Nu frowned at the question. "He did not attend his lessons yesterday morning, but I thought it was simply a lad playing hooky."

"He had done that before?" the singer asked—a very good question.

Master Nu shook his head. "Not him, but many others had. I thought it was simply his turn."

The singer nodded, a soft smile on his lips. "I remember as a boy sitting in lessons and wishing only to be out on the lake. The monastery and its rules were so stifling." He shrugged. "I grew up at Inle Lake and was a novice at Inle monastery."

Master Nu nodded. "We were as young once. That is why I tolerate their absences. If they are hungry for their studies, they will come back. Being the only boy who cannot read or write is not a distinction most of them want. And in the meantime, Buddha's teachings sink in more than they realize."

"The rules of society." The old singer nodded.

"You can say that, yes."

"Do you have any idea where Hlaing Htay might have gone when playing hooky?"

Master Nu shook his head, but looked off toward the river as if he would not meet the singer's gaze. Interesting. Was Master Nu hiding something?

"Where do the novices usually go when they play hooky?"

Master Nu shrugged. "I spent my novice years here and have never left. For me, study was a calling. But others of my friends loved to go to the river. They would swim and spend time with the children of the raftmen bringing logs downriver."

Not something approved of apparently.

"Would it be possible to speak to Hlaing Htay's friends? They may know where the boy went and why,"the old singer asked.

Master Nu hesitated. "Why are you so interested? Should it not be the authorities asking?"

And you, Yamin wanted to say. Don't you want to know what happened, too? But he held his opinions to himself, biting the inside of his mouth to remind himself.

Sighing, the old singer shook his head. "Nai Naing, the headman, has made it clear that we are to investigate. He wants no part of the matter."

Old Master Nu's gaze narrowed, but then he nodded. "No, I suppose he would not. Then it seems I must find the boys for you. I should say that young Lwin Kwye missed his lessons this morning. Those two boys were always glued together. I had not thought anything of it—until now. Now I am worried."

The old singer tensed. His grip tightened on Yamin. "Who were their friends? Find them for me, now! We don't know what happened to Hlaing Htay, but we don't want something similar befalling Lwin Kwye!"

The singer's urgency must have been evident to Master Nu. He nodded and motioned the old singer to follow.

He led the old singer past the dormitory and around the main temple to old, walled gardens that held carved likenesses of heavenly apsaras dancing in between rough patches of stone. The garden was filled with banana palms and lines of washing. A paso was spread on the earth with cooked rice drying in the sun—the morning offerings to be saved against a day of greater hunger, perhaps. It would be fun to leave footprints in the grains and wait for the monks' reaction. Hmm.

Beyond the lines of clothing, a grassy area overlooked the glistening back of the great river. There, twelve young monks were seated in a circle facing an ancient monk.

"What must we recognize when we suffer?" the old monk asked in a voice like the wind whispering through grass.

"That all life is suffering?" said one round-faced lad.

"Is that an answer or a question?" the old monk asked seriously, but the sunlight caught the twinkle in his eye.

"An—an answer?" The moon-faced lad responded.

The old monk frowned. "You must be certain, youngsters. Always you must be certain that life brings suffering, but what else did Buddha teach?" He scanned his young audience, who remained silent, so Yamin wanted to leap up and yell, "All things pass away, even suffering!"

But he remembered himself and held still.

"Perhaps the youngsters should be tasked with thinking about the answer," Master Nu said to the teacher. "Before you are so tasked, who here has seen Lwin Kwye today?"

The youngsters looked at each other, but shook their heads.

"He was gone when I rose this morning," volunteered the moon-faced lad. "I thought he had gone to the latrine, but he hasn't returned."

"Who were Lwin Kwye and Hlaing Htay's best friends?" the old singer asked.

The boys looked at each other again and then at their hands, all except one skinny boy who looked close to tears.

"They were always closest to each other," said the thin lad. His cheek bore a birthmark shaped like a Yamin-sized hand.

"No one else?"

"Bo," the old monk said in his whispery voice. "Didn't you help Lwin Kwye and Hlaing Htay with chores yesterday? I believe you were to sweep the temple grounds." He picked up an old banana leaf that had fallen to the ground near him. "Perhaps you did not complete the task?"

Bo was apparently the thin youngster Yamin had spotted. The boy swallowed hard, but nodded. "We swept around the temple buildings. Hlaing Htay did not think you meant for us to sweep this far."

"There. There is the one for you to interview," Master Nu said.

The old singer nodded, but stepped past the monk to speak to the boys. "You are novices together. You entered the monastery together and yet you were not friends?"

Again, the young monks stirred like leaves caught in a slight wind—as if a sigh had rippled through them. The old singer was onto something.

"They—they were different. Not from Pagan town," the moon-faced boy finally said. The echoing nods around the group said he was their spokesman. "They were from the villages northward. They stuck together."

And you stuck together and excluded them, just like the royal puppets in the troupe excluded him, the one who annoyed them, Yamin thought. It was most unfair—something a kind person would not do. He looked at the bright faces of the youngsters and for a moment saw something darker and unpleasant in them. And here he'd thought favorably of human children...

The old monk closed his eyes and without their twinkle it was almost possible to think he was dead. Then he drew in a heavy sigh. "I am troubled at you boys. This is a community. As novices you are all equal here. You were to leave the world of town and village behind and be here—in this moment, in this place. Instead you brought the outside with you."

"And one of you is dead," the old singer said.

"What?" The boys' voices were a shrill chorus that the singer ignored.

"Bo and you," the singer said and pointed at the moon-faced boy who seemed inclined to talk. "Come with me."

The boys scrambled up.

"I would use your meeting room to interview these two," the singer said.

Master Nu led them to the monastery and up the many teak stairs into a broad room unlike any Yamin had ever entered. Yoke thei were not usually taken to monastery temples.

The walls were age-and-incense smoke-darkened wood, with windows that stretched from a man's waist up to the ceiling. Each window had broad double doors now open to the sunlight, but even with the columns of light flooding in, the beamed ceiling was dim and so was the oversized altar where a ten-foot-tall, lonely-looking alabaster Buddha sat with his hands in the *touching-the-earth* mudra with one hand open on his lap and the other hand stretched down with fingers grazing the ground. The statue's benign face gazed over the silent empty floorboards, showing his commitment to the enlightenment he had found. The enlightenment that the old singer wished to pursue and that a killer clearly had turned away from.

Yamin stiffened at the deep thought. Deep thoughts were not something he was used to. It felt too big for his head and made his chest tight as if everything inside had turned frothy and was overflowing. He tore his gaze away from the Buddha just as Master Nu asked whether this room would do.

"It will serve nicely, thank you." The singer cradled Yamin uncomfortably in the crook of an elbow as he pressed his palms together and bowed. Then he motioned the two boys to be seated and turned back to the waiting monk. "I would interview them alone, thank you."

A Death in Passing

For a moment Master Nu looked as if he would protest, but then he nodded and left the room.

Yamin inhaled the scent of the marigolds draped on the lap of the Buddha. Before the statue, a water bowl held lotus blossoms, the pale green buds just nearing opening.

"Well." The old singer settled himself on the floor. He settled Yamin seated by his knee and it was terribly hard to hold to his pretend wood when the boys stared at him. What would they do if he stuck out his tongue? Perhaps he could roll his eyes and make them wonder whether they had seen it. But the old singer had said he should not move...

Ohhh, it was so tempting!

"What is your name, lad?" the old singer asked the moon-faced boy.

"Chit, sir." The lad would not meet the singer's gaze, but he snuck peeks in Yamin's direction every few moments. "Is that a royal puppet?" The question seemed to burst from his lips.

The singer nodded. "In fact it is. This is Yamin and I have brought him with me because he is my assistant. Leastways he sings the best songs for our audience and I thought the people might like to meet him."

He did? They would?

The old singer smiled at the two young boys. At the old singer's words the two youngsters seemed to relax and lean forward to look more openly at Yamin. After all, a page would be a very good playmate for young humans such as these.

Yamin held his peace as the old singer continued.

"It is nice to meet you, Chit. I'd like to know everything you can tell me about Hlaing Htay and Lwin Kwye. What were they like? Who did they like to talk to? Who were their friends? Where did they like to go?"

Chit glanced at Bo as if waiting for the other boy to say something. Then he looked at Yamin with something akin to longing. "I have always wanted to see a royal puppet troupe. I think Hlaing Htay felt the same way. We discussed it once... before..."

"Before what?" the singer asked.

"You know—before we got to know each other. Before I didn't like him anymore."

Pursing his lips, the old singer sat back. "That is too bad. It is never nice to not like someone. What happened?"

Moon-faced Chit shrugged. "It was nothing. He just—he wasn't my kind?"

"A poor boy from the country?"

Chit squirmed where he sat. "Not poor. He just—he believed silly things."

The old singer said nothing and the silence stretched until Yamin found his patience straining. Finally, Chit broke the impasse. "He believed in spirits—that there are spirits in the trees, in the rocks, in the hills." Chit shook his head and puffed himself up. "How can anyone believe such foolishness?"

Because...because I'm such a spirit! The words pressed up the back of Yamin's throat until the singer placed a gentle hand on his shoulder.

"Perhaps he knew something you didn't," the singer said softly.

The boy must have seen something in the old singer's face, for he frowned. "Surely you cannot believe. You've been so many places. You must have seen..." Then his gaze widened. "No..."

Yamin felt the old singer nod. "I have seen many strange things in my travels. The spirits—the nats—are just part of them. They inhabit everything."

"You've seen them?" Chit asked.

"And at times, spoken with them. They are unruly creatures and usually not to be trusted, but they do exist."

Capricious was the term that Min Mahagiri, the king of nats, had used. It was such a lovely word the way it rolled on the tongue.

"So the town boys did not accept Hlaing Htay or Lwin Kwye because they believed in the old faith. Do I have the right of it?"

Chit hung his head. "We teased them about it. They did not like it. They used to go off together to get away from us. We used to say it was to pray to little men who lived in the rocks and grass."

"I see." The old singer held the boy in his gaze and then turned to Bo, huddled by the window ledge. "Is that how it was?"

The boy nodded miserably. "They believed. They talked about the wonderful things that the spirits did, like Boun Magyi, the rice mother, making the rice fields grow and Min Mahagiri keeping everyone safe at his home. I—I wanted to believe..."

"But sometimes it is hard to believe when other friends say the truth isn't so. Did your teacher tell you that we each live in our own small prison of truth? What we choose to believe means that we turn our backs on so many other ways to look at the world. For each of us, what we believe becomes our world, but who is to say which truth is reality?"

Bo nodded slowly. "Master Nu says that there is no reality. The world is all our imagination and will pass away."

"Very true. So where did Hlaing Htay and Lwin Kwye like to go in their reality?"

The two boys looked at each other as if they shared a secret. Finally Bo sighed and his shoulders slumped.

"I took them there once. To Thatbyinnyu Pahto. They always talked about the temples they climbed around their village."

"They always acted as if they thought they were better that the rest of us because they'd climbed to the top," Chit said, nodding.

"I—I pretended to be their friend and they took me with them once. They went out into a field and climbed one of the small brick pahtos right to the top. They were very good using their fingers and toes and climbed up it like monkeys. I did it, too. It was— difficult."

The two boys looked at each other again and Yamin knew something more had happened. The old singer simply waited.

"When we got back, I told Chit and the others. We laughed at Hlaing Htay and Lwin Kwye to their faces and told them they were not even good monkeys until they climbed one of the large temples in Pagan. That was where the real pahtos were. So we took them to Thatbyinnyu and told them to climb it if they wanted to prove something."

The teak monastery was silent save for the sound of the old singer's breathing and the sound of monk's voices from the kitchens beyond. The scent of steaming rice came through the window as did the hum of the river. Even Yamin could feel the old singer's disapproval.

"What did they do?" the old singer asked.

"They tried to climb it, but they couldn't. Everyone knows that Thatbyinnyu is not like the old walls around the monastery that old Master Nu wants to rebuild. The bricks are so well laid at Thatbyinnyu that it is barely possible to poke a piece of grass between them."

"So you gave them a task they could not perform?" the singer asked.

"We wanted to show them that they were not so special," Chit said.

"I see. And what happened after that?"

"They did not talk about it anymore," Chit said.

"But that wasn't the end," Bo interrupted. "They were always disappearing, so I followed them one day. They didn't go to Thatbyinnyu, but to Dhammayangyi Pahto." His face crinkled as if he did not like the place. "They were climbing there. I watched for a while and then came home. They were very good."

"You didn't tell us that," Chit said.

Bo's gaze fell. "I—I thought we should leave them in peace. If they wanted to believe themselves great climbers, what harm did it do? They were not talking to us about it anymore."

"You left them to climb one of the large temples and did not tell anyone?"

Bo shrugged miserably. "I—I told myself that if they got hurt no one would care."

Yamin pressed back against the old singer's thigh, reassessing everything he'd thought about playing with these young humans. Great Nat save him from the friendship of a human boy.

Chapter 6

The sun was falling toward afternoon when Aung left the boys in Master Nu's hands at the monastery. Pagan town was full of people—almost as many as at Popa—but these were people going about their business, not consumed with revelry as at the mountain festival. Since he had been here last on business, the town had grown with new houses. Some were of an Amarapura style but had large, ornate nat houses by their front gates—something seen far less in the capital city where the king had outlawed the propitiating of the nats. Perhaps people were moving here from the city to get away from the king's strictures.

As he passed through town he came upon a shop with a man carving the lintels of a roof, a half-built nat house beside him in front of his workshop. The sweet spice of teak wood filled the air.

"I think I see your work in front of many of the town's newest houses," Aung said and bowed his head in greeting.

The man glanced up from his carving. "What? Are you, also, going to tell me that nat houses are not wanted?"

Aung was surprised. "I was admiring your fine work. Are there others who dislike it?"

The carver looked up and laid his hand on the small carved building beside him. Each corner pillar was carved like fish scales, and flowers were fashioned at the corners of the eaves. The house was perhaps two feet high, but stood on its post, it topped Aung's head. When he was done, it would provide a home for the nat spirits who protected the owner's house. The small figure of the nat would stand within the open walls and offerings would be made by the owner to keep the nat happy and helpful.

"You're not from here. You're one of the puppeteers that came into town last night." He lifted his chin. "That one of them? I hear they're finely made. Any chance I could have a look at him?"

Aung stepped back and tightened his hold on Yamin. The little page might stand for a lot, but he certainly would not stand for that. Aung shook his head.

"These are royal yoke thei. They are handled only by their puppeteers." And him apparently, though it really was unheard of. He must ask Yamin why he allowed it.

The carver shook his head and continued carefully sculpting the upswept edges of the roof. "Too bad."

"You mentioned others did not approve of your work?"

The carver shrugged. "There's a few who follow the king's edicts in town, or use the king's edicts as an excuse not to do their duty. Not to mention a few of those foreign types always preaching about their god. There's been nat houses destroyed so the folks come to me. It's good for business, I suppose."

Aung thanked him for his time and continued on his way, but U Myint caught up to them. "Singer! I've asked around about the nuns but there is no one who knows them north of town."

Aung nodded and considered the news. "The boy lives this way, but I'm told his best friend, a lad named Lwin Kwye, is also missing. Could you please ask for aid from the troupe and try to find him? I fear for his safety."

U Myint looked at him gravely. "You think the boys may have both happened upon a misadventure?"

Sighing, Aung shook his head. "I'm told both boys like to climb Dhammayangyi Pahto—where we found the dead lad. Perhaps they happened upon someone or something they shouldn't have seen when up at the heights..."

U Myint went thoughtful. "There are too many ill things in this world, it seems." He turned a misty gaze on Aung. Clearly the loss of the garuda still haunted him. Though not a major puppet, the mighty garuda bird was the steed of the king of the gods and a very great loss to the troupe. "I will alert the others and see what I can find."

He left, his hurried footfall leaving a cloud of red dust rising behind him.

Aung glanced down at Yamin and sighed once more. "Things are changing, Yamin. I fear there is a battle mounting over the hearts and minds of the Burmese people."

But Yamin wisely did not respond. There were too many people still around, though they had left the main areas of Pagan town in search of the dead boy's village.

North of the center of Pagan town, the stilted houses quickly gave way to fields that awaited the rains. When they came, pale rice shoots would poke their heads above the water, and the reflected sky would fill the area for a short time. Along the river, soapberry and htaung trees hung dusty branches. Thorn brush grew up by the road. Here and there small herds of goats nibbled at the brush and at the dried-out stalks of old grass that edged the fields.

Small copses of trees—toddy palm, mango, and neem—provided shade for tiny villages of no more than three or four dwellings that housed the farmers who worked these fields and the dry fields that would hold dry rice and wheat after the rains.

He stopped at one such village and got directions to Hlaing Htay's home in one of twin villages that sat north and inland from the river. It was a long hour's walk northward under a leaden sun and Aung felt his strength fading as he followed the dusty path into the village. It was clearly not a wealthy place. Five small, stilted, bamboo houses sat around a common dirt area, their thatched palm roofs dried golden by the sun. But though the houses were lowly, the place was clean, the common area swept bare of all leaves. The small cooking hearths lay ready for cooking the evening meal. Fifteen people crowded around one of the houses. Most were women and children, except for a wizened grandfather. The old man sported a wispy beard and loosely wound blue turban and blue paso tucked up between his spindly legs as farmers were wont to do.

To Aung the old man turned a brown gaze that was bluing with age. "You have come, then. I told them you would."

Aung frowned. "How could you know I was coming? I just decided myself."

The old man nodded. "When they brought my grandson's body home, they told me he had been found by the royal puppet troupe—the same who caught a killer at Mount Popa. I told my daughter that you would not let my grandson's soul wander to become a hungry ghost."

He glanced at the house. "It is more than the monks would do. They have only sent one monk to pray over Hlaing Htay's body. How can that be enough to ease his fury and pain? Should an innocent like him be forced to wander an eternity, hungry for life?"

Aung shook his head no. "I am Aung Aung, the Master Singer," he said and half bowed.

The old man's brows rose. "Even before Popa I had heard of your prowess. I am Khun Win. I attended one of your troupe's performances years ago. Your words were so clever they made me cry laughing—at the expense of the king, I might add." He bowed to Aung with his hands palms-together before his face, as one might bow to his better.

Aung sighed. "I am sorry about your grandson. I wanted to speak with his family to find out about him. What kind of boy was he? Did he have enemies? Close friends?"

Even as he asked it, he doubted the question's worth. Who would hate enough to kill a ten-year-old?

"Your grandson was found far from where he should have been," Aung continued. "Apparently he and another boy have been attempting to climb the outside of the Dhammayangyi Pahto, but he was not found outside. He had not fallen."

Khun Win nodded. "By the marks on his body he was strangled, his neck broken."

"Broken!" Aung was surprised that he had not noticed. "Why would someone kill your grandson?"

Khun Win looked away, his paling gaze brimming with tears he would not cry, for *bhammasan chin* said you did not show such strong emotion. "My grandson was a good boy—typical of his age. He could be an apsara and a scamp, a hellion and prince—much like that little page you hold." He shook his head. "I loved him. He was my youngest grandson and he would spend hours at my knee asking for stories of the old ways and the heroes and the nats. In my old age he was my comfort—always tending to an old man's needs so that I was sorry to see him go to the monastery, but go he must. To become a good man, he must learn the truth of the world."

"I am told he had only one friend amongst the novitiates," Aung said.

"Lwin Kwye. He is a good lad from the next village." He nodded at the twin village across the fields. "The two have played together since they were very young."

"Now Lwin Kwye is missing—just as Hlaing Htay was missed before his body was found. Can you think of anyone who might wish to harm both the boys?"

Khun Win turned a devastated face to Aung. "My grandson is dead and now you tell me my cousin's grandson may be as well?" He staggered and Aung caught his elbow and helped him to sit. Aung had forgotten how family lines intertwined across the landscape of villages.

Khun Win scrambled up quickly and looked to the house. "I must help my daughter. Stop this from happening again. No one should feel such suffering, no matter what Buddha says!"

He pulled away from Aung and pushed in amongst the crowd of women and youngsters. Aung stood there, feeling the waves of pain come off the crowd. Hlaing Htay might have been the youngest, but perhaps he held the hearts the greatest.

A pinch from Yamin brought him back to himself. For a moment he'd forgotten the page was fully aware. "There!" Yamin whispered. "By the corner of the house."

Aung casually let his gaze float over the gathering. A movement at the corner of the house caught his eye, but by the time he turned his attention, it was gone. The pillar that held up the house stood by itself.

"You missed him." Yamin clearly disapproved.

There was nothing Aung could do about that. Instead he caught the eye of a young man who was close to Thura's seventeen years and motioned him over. The young man reluctantly left his family.

Aung introduced himself and the young man bowed deeply.

"I am Khin Moe, Hlaing Htay's cousin. How can I help so illustrious a man?"

Aung half bowed at the compliment. "I—we— are investigating the death of your cousin and I need to know everything there is to know about him. Did you know Hlaing Htay well?"

Khin Moe gave a disarming grin. "As well as brothers might. After my mother's death, I lived with Hlaing Htay's family while my father was traveling— until I was old enough to go with him. He is a tinker. I am learning the trade, though with the new pots now flooding in from Yangoon, who is to say how long we'll be needed?" He said it proudly, with a hint of anger, and his muscled physique said he had the strength to pound tin and copper into pots and pans for sale.

"What kind of lad was he?" Aung asked.

Khin Moe shrugged. "About like most. He could get under your skin as most boys do—too full of himself from time to time. But he had a kindly heart."

The latter was said as if he had learned the phrase by rote. "His mother thought that, I'm sure," Aung said. "What did you think?"

Surprise glimmered in Khin Moe's gaze for a moment, to be followed by a glimpse of something else. Anger?

At Hlaing Htay or at Aung for asking the question?

"Of course he was kind, but he could also be a stinker from time to time. He told my father that I was thinking of leaving the business."

Clearly this was a point of some importance. "Was it true?"

Khin Moe nodded. "Of course it was true. That didn't mean that my father had to know. It caused friction between us that need not have been."

"So you were angry with Hlaing Htay?"

Khin Moe stiffened and drew himself up to his full height so that for a moment Aung felt threatened. The young man was taller and brawnier than all of the puppeteers and musicians save for Nyein, the dragon drummer.

"Angry? Yes. Angry enough to kill my cousin-brother? Never."

Aung bowed his head. "Were there other people he infuriated?"

"How about everybody? He would not help his father in the fields because he preferred to sit with his grandfather and listen to old tales. His mother he tormented with his desires. The other youngsters found him boring. I've heard even his teachers at the monastery did not care for him."

This was a far cry from what he had heard from Master Nu, but Aung carefully kept his face neutral. "Was there anyone in particular who might have threatened the boy?"

Khin Moe thought a moment. "Not that I heard. The only threats were that he be placed in the monastery. He did not like the thought of the work, nor of the fasting."

"But then, what lad does, neh?" Aung said, to test Khin Moe's attitude, for truly most boys tested their novitiate vows. A much younger Aung certainly had.

After a brief pause, the young man nodded. "It is typical, I suppose."

Aung turned to look across the fields to the sister village. "Are Lwin Kwye's parents at home?"

"Lwin Kwye? What do you want with him?" Khin Moe asked.

"He has disappeared just as Hlaing Htay did before he was found dead. I hoped to speak to them."

Khin Moe glanced from the village under its swaying toddy palms and back to the houseful of mourners. "They are already here comforting Hlaing Htay's parents," he whispered.

Aung considered calling them out to question them, but he could not bring himself to cause more pain. Their interview could wait another day and hopefully the lad would be found safe by then. He thanked Khin Moe and excused himself. The low murmur of the monk's prayers came from the inside of the house. Out in one of the dry fields, the village's men built a pyre. For fear of hungry ghosts, the boy's body would be burned as soon as possible.

Aung only prayed to find the killer before another pyre was necessary.

§

The light faded on the long walk home. The stars had come out over the eastern edge of the world, though the far west still blushed the red of Minthamee's cheeks when she was in the Mintha's arms. Yamin wondered what it would be like to love like that, because from the outside it had seemed entirely boring. Perhaps if you *felt* it, the boringness would not be so evident. An interesting thought, for from what he'd seen of human love, it could get you killed and it could leave you grieving. No...love was not something he was certain he wanted to try.

Mysteries, however—they were never boring. The breeze was pleasantly cool and around them stretched the dusty farmlands with the ancient brick towers that stuck out like twenty- and thirty-foot fingers poking here and there through the landscape. In the failing light the bricks were black, save for the red gleam on one side from the dying sunlight. It was altogether a grim scene—as if the land itself was in the throes of dying.

"I, myself, am not partial to this place," he said, struggling to sit up in the old singer's arms.

"Shh. Be still," the old singer said.

"Why? Is there someone about?" Yamin craned his head and when the singer tried to force him back into his 'in-his-wood' position, Yamin jerked loose and leapt to the ground. "Really, singer. Am I to just be luggage carted around? You won't speak to me at the puppet camp for fear of the giant. You won't speak to me here in case of anyone else. What are you hiding? Have you decided we are not partners in these investigations?" Because if the old man had made that decision, Yamin wasn't telling him what he had seen. He'd conduct his *own* investigation and show the old singer up. After all, Yamin had noticed things at the dead boy's home that the old singer apparently hadn't seen.

He glared up at the singer with his arms crossed over his chest and his toes tapping. The singer really had made him most cross at the moment.

The old singer sighed and ran his boney fingers back under his turban. "Truly I am sorry, Yamin. I was deep in thought and hadn't even noticed there was no one around." He motioned at the almost total darkness lit only by the distant cook fires and torches of Pagan town. "We will have our discussion here, as you suggest." He scanned the eastern horizon. "The moon will be rising soon. We'll start walking again at moonrise."

Yamin led the old singer off the road to a copse of htaung trees with one fragrant neem tree heavy with yellow flowers, where they settled onto the earth that was littered with fading blossoms. A dove coo-cooed at their presence and then settled back in the branches. The stars spread over the sky like a carpet awaiting the moon's arrival.

"So what do you think, Yamin? Who are our suspects? My head aches with trying to sort through it all." The singer rubbed his bushy brows and pressed the bridge of his nose as if he was afraid all his thoughts would spill out. He looked—not tired like had always looked after physical effort—but weary. Yes, that was the word.

But at least he was finally asking what Yamin thought.

"Well, I still would bet on the giant. He might have been fighting the brigands, but he could have committed the murder before."

"But what would be his motivation, Yamin? Why would he kill a boy?"

Yamin thought a moment. "Isn't that what giants *do*? Aren't they *evil*?"

The old singer peered down at him, backlit by stars. "But he is not actually a giant. He is just a human who is very tall. Many of the foreigners are, you know."

"Then I shouldn't like to live amongst them at all," Yamin said with a shake of his head. "It would hurt my neck looking up at them."

"They would not believe you are alive. They would keep you in a box to look at, and that is all."

Yamin's heart beat a little harder. "It sounds like a prison," he whispered. No place he wanted to be, that was certain. A wicker basket was a much more attractive alternative.

"All right. If not the giant, then how about those young monks," said Yamin. "They were very evil to Hlaing Htay and Lwin Kwye and they still did not like them."

The old singer nodded. "That is true, but would a child actually kill another child? It is a possibility I pray is not true. Besides, we were told Hlaing Htay's neck was broken. I do not believe the boys would have the strength to do such a thing."

That made sense, even if those boys were fiends. "So adults, then."

"Or boys much older."

"You mean Khin Moe, the cousin?" Yamin thought of the young man the singer had spoken to. "You are right. He did not seem over-fond of Hlaing Htay."

The old singer nodded. "Apparently our victim liked telling tales about people. That sort of thing could make enemies."

"Like Master Nu," Yamin said, thinking of the teaching master. The monk had seemed like a nice enough human as humans went, but then Yamin had discovered that judging human niceness was not something he was particularly good at. "I heard what the cousin said. And Master Nu was not particularly helpful. Did you notice that he avoided most questions about Hlaing Htay and was more concerned for Lwin Kwye?"

Nodding, the singer thought a moment. "That is most likely out of concern for Lwin Kwye's safety. He already knew Hlaing Htay was dead. There was nothing he could do for him."

"He could have answered your questions better!" Yamin said. Wasn't the singer listening?

"He is a monk, Yamin. A senior monk and well regarded enough to be in charge of teaching the novices. What motive would he have to kill one of his charges?"

In frustration Yamin blew a breath up over his forehead and fingered the edge of his vest. "All right. What about the brigands? Or maybe Lwin Kwye killed his friend and that is why he is hiding?"

The old singer looked momentarily shocked. "You have a most distrusting mind, my small friend. Most distrusting. Next you will tell me it could be one of our troupe."

"Nooo!" Yamin shook his head. "But you make me think. The people around here seem to know of us and that we would be coming. They had heard of our mystery in Popa. That says to me that many pilgrims have traveled through this place before us. Perhaps one of them committed the deed."

Nodding, the old singer looked troubled. "That thought has crossed my mind as well, but again I come back to motive. As we discovered on Popa, motive is everything. People do not kill for the fun of it."

Yamin wasn't so sure given what he'd seen and heard in his two previous adventures and this investigation wasn't allaying his impressions. "So? What motivations are there to kill a young monk?"

"A very good question, indeed, my friend. What do you think?"

"Well... from what the two young monks said, Hlaing Htay and Lwin Kwye were probably going to succeed in scaling the Pahto. That would make the other boys more foolish looking and would make Hlaing Htay and Lwin Kwye seem brave."

"So jealousy could be a motive," the singer said, nodding. "Yes, that is a very old motive. Go on, Yamin. You are proving very perceptive."

As if that was a surprise! If anyone had asked, he could have told them that he was always *very* perceptive—given half a chance.

He scratched the base of a ponytail. Hmm. "The cousin said that Hlaing Htay made enemies because he talked too much. Perhaps he talked one too many times."

Overhead, bats' wings made designs against the stars and their soft cries filled the sky. In the dim light, the old singer rubbed his chin. Finally he nodded. "Often adults pay no mind to a youngster in their midst, so they speak as if the youngster is not there. Hlaing Htay may have overhead something and threatened to tell the tale. Fear of the release of this information could lead to a killing. But what did he hear? Who in a place like Pagan town could have said something terrible enough to warrant killing?" He shook his head. "That is something we will need to learn. We must keep our eyes and ears open for secrets, Yamin. Someone had a secret that has devoured the soul inside him. He may live, but he is already a hungry ghost."

As if in answer, a ghostly glow filled the sky in the east. Both of them turned to watch as the moon rose, bringing with it the old man that the kindly moon had rescued from loneliness. It was hard to imagine being old and lonely when you had thirty-six brethren carved from the same tree, but then the old singer had seemed quite lonely until Yamin had become determined to work with him. Now Yamin made sure that he spoke with the old singer every day. There was no way the singer could be lonely, and if he was not lonely, surely he would put away thoughts of retiring to a monastery in his home village.

At least that was the hope. They would never investigate so well if the two of them were not together.

When the moon's almost round face was fully risen, the singer stood to the cracking of his joints. "Come, Yamin. We must get back to the others and you must not be seen as living. By the way, it seems that there will be a performance tomorrow. Zeya will likely want to practice."

Yamin resented the fact that the old singer had made the decision to leave before Yamin had had the chance to talk about what he had seen at the village. Then he sighed and held up his arms for the singer for the long walk home. There would be another time to tell the singer—if he decided to share the information. In the meantime there was another performance. More of the strings. For all he liked the songs the old singer made for him, he was getting sorely tired of being a puppeteer's plaything. He and the other yoke thei were not much more than children to the puppeteers—something to be pushed around and overlooked or ignored most of the time—except when a performance rolled around. For the other yoke thei, it seemed to be fine—they preferred to while away their time in the cloud fields of the north.

Yamin frowned, for it no longer felt good to him. Then he remembered to paste his smile on his face.

Chapter 7

The moon was high in the heavens when Aung staggered into the puppet troupe's camping spot, but there were no wicker trunks, no sleeping mats, and no lounging puppeteers and musicians. Only a small fire where Thura waited. Aung's heart fluttered in his chest. Had Saya Lin finally given up on his singer and left for Yangoon?

Around the campsite the grass was flattened where the wicker trunks had waited, while the wind rustled the tall stalks around the bases of the derelict temples. Beyond Thura, the space that Harold Heath had occupied was also empty. His horse was gone and the space that had been filled with the animal's contented munching was now filled by the murmur of the river. The air was damp from the river water and from the clouds that scuttled northward, masking the southern cross and the face of the old man in the moon.

Aung stopped and settled Yamin to the ground as if he was wood. "So. Has Saya Lin decided to leave without me, then?" Given the schism between them, it was a believable possibility, though it pained him greatly.

Thura shook his head. "He would not leave without you—or our friend here." Thura nodded down at Yamin. "He is too important to the troupe."

As opposed to an old singer who could be, and should be, replaced.

"They've gone to another location for the merchant's pwe. Saya Lin left me to guide you there."

"And the foreigner?"

Thura shook his head. "Saya Lin said that given the man had not stolen from us, he was free to go."

"Free to go!" Yamin leapt up. "He let a giant go loose?"

"Shh!" Both Thura and Aung leaned down to the little page and Aung picked him up again. "This place is too close to too many houses, Yamin. You must remain in your wood."

"It's not fair! It's just not fair the way you always push me around, singer!" The little page struggled in his arms. "I am not some plaything to be shoved about with strings! I might look a boy, but I am far more!"

"And I am truly aware, Yamin. I once made the error of thinking you a child, but I have put that perception behind me. You have a keen mind—keener than many a human's. But please. It is too dangerous to have these conversations here."

What had gotten into the little page? He might be difficult, but this—this anger—was not like him.

Yamin was positively trembling in his hands.

"Please, Yamin. Believe me." He held the page loosely and let him decide how to deal with the situation. Finally Yamin heaved a great sigh and sagged against Aung's shoulder.

"I don't want to be a boy, a child, for eternity," Yamin whispered.

"Oh, Yamin," Aung whispered back, into the little one's ear. "And I would wish to be as young as that again. How different we are."

It was something Aung brooded on as he held Yamin to him and allowed Thura to lead them from the open field by the river and back amid the dark brick mountains that were the great temples of Pagan.

§

The troupe was camped in the walled courtyard of a great temple that lifted many tiers to a great corncob peak that seemed to reach up to the sky. The troupe had already constructed their stage against a walled corner so that there was only a small space where they hung curtains to protect the troupe from prying eyes. Yamin took it all in as the old singer set him down.

The walls were gray stone that glowed softly in the moonlight just like the stone of the massive temple that loomed over them. A neem tree leaned over the wall and had sprinkled the earth with scented flowers that stuck to his toes as he took in his surroundings. The camp smelled of rice and fish, so clearly the evening meal had been eaten. To one side, the wicker trunks had been opened. The yoke thei filled their wood again.

There was the Thagyar Min—the celestial king—standing cross-armed and surveilling his domain while he awaited the moment to make his predictions for the year. At the base of their trunks, the dead Min's courtiers huddled talking in quiet voices about whatever it was that had kept them occupied all these centuries. For a moment Yamin wondered. And there was lovely Minthamee complaining about the state of her clothes and hair, though clearly her puppeteer had already labored long to fix the pearls and jewels that had come loose from her clothing during the giant's fight with the brigands. She stood, complaining, on her basket with her arms akimbo as the puppeteer labored over her. The naga serpent rattled his scales. The white horse trotted around the curtained area as if it was a paddock designed for a horse to stretch its legs. The monkey chittered and threw the fallen neem blossoms at anyone who came near.

And instead of feeling like he was home amongst his kin, he felt he was some spare part that no one noticed. None of the other yoke thei even acknowledged him, and the humans—well, except for Zeya—were all too busy for him. Zeya hurried up.

"There you are! I was getting worried that something might have happened. Master Aung really shouldn't take you away for so long. It's a big world out there for one so small."

He gathered Yamin up without even asking.

"Stop!" Yamin said, struggling to free himself. "I am not an inanimate object. I have two legs that I enjoy using even if you insist in carrying me in a box."

He leapt down to the ground and glared up at Zeya, who stared back at him with wide eyes.

"Do not pick me up again unless we have agreed on it."

The young puppeteer finally nodded. "You surprise me, Yamin. I never knew you minded." He set off across the enclosure and Yamin followed.

Frankly, he hadn't known he minded, either. Was it possible that the whole world was changing around him and as a result he was changing, too? The thought was horrifying. What would he change into? Caterpillars became butterflies, but he already had yoke thei wings when not in his wood. Most other creatures kept the same form—they just got bigger.

Now there was a grand thought—a Yamin big as the giant. Then no one could ignore him anymore.

At his basket Zeya fussed over his clothing and his hair. The final straw was when Zeya admonished him to quit scratching at his ponytails because it mussed his hair.

It felt as if something inside him burst. He ripped away from Zeya, leapt off his trunk, and turned. "I will scratch my head whenever I want! I will tug at my vest when I want. I might even roll in the dirt—if I want. And you—you will quit ordering me around. All of you!" He pointed at the puppet troupe. "Do you understand? I am not a child's toy. I am yoke thei—living and breathing— and I belong to *me*!" He plopped down cross-legged on the ground with his back to the lot of them. The wall of the courtyard became suddenly very interesting with its smooth parts and rough broken niches.

"Yamin, I am most sorry if I have distressed you. If I have disrespected you..." Zeya plucked at Yamin's shoulder.

"Leave me alone. You're only concerned because Saya Lin will be angry if you cannot dance me. Apparently, I can't leave because it might cause the end of the world if someone saw me, but I will ask you to just let me be alone."

He heard Zeya's breathing behind him, then his footfalls leaving. Yamin sighed and rested his chin in his hands. Why, oh, why did he just feel like crying—like the entire world was pressing in on him and he did not like the world very much today. Not a world where even the children were evil to each other.

He sighed again. All these years he had been performing for the children—to make them laugh. He had loved their pure, honest laughter, but it turned out that it wasn't pure at all. They were mean-spirited little humans who, given time, would grow into mean-spirited large humans—that was all.

"Yamin?" the old singer asked softly. "May I join you?"

He nodded and, with a crunching of joints, the old singer sat cross-legged beside him. He motioned someone else—by the sound of his breathing, most likely Zeya—to leave.

"You've got young Zeya very worried, my small friend."

Yamin cringed at being reminded of his size. "I don't care if he worries. I'm fine. I just don't want to do things his way all the time. Or yours, for that matter."

He glanced sideways at the singer to gauge his reaction.

A small smile curved the old singer's lips.

"Are you laughing at me?" Yamin asked.

"Not at all. I was just thinking how I have always thought that you did most whatever you wanted to do. You certainly don't always do as you're told. You would not be Yamin if you did. Do you remember how you took it upon yourself to watch the Queens' house, even though I told you not to? I had no idea that you could do so without being noticed, but you did. And there were times that I told you to stay home, and yet you were there to lead me when darkness blinded these old eyes of mine. I am here to admit that there were times I was wrong and you were right to do things your way."

Yamin swallowed the confusing emotions that were threatening to overwhelm him. "You really think so?"

"I know so. You have been a most able investigator and we could not have solved the past two crimes if we did not work together. All of us—all of the troupe—know that, but it does not make it any easier to break from the traditions. You—you are unique amongst the yoke thei, my friend. It will just take time for all of us to understand it and what it means."

"But what does it mean, singer? I am trapped by my appearance so that everyone forgets what I am, and with all that I am learning, I find that I am learning to unlike humans. How can I perform for people I do not like?"

The singer seemed to consider for a moment. "As a species I suppose there are many things not to like, but I know that you like Zeya. You told me so, yourself. You said he is jolly. And I think you like Thura for his voice. And I hope you like me, just a little, after all that we have done together."

Yamin swallowed and nodded. It was all true, except he like the old singer most of all, for he had believed that a small page could investigate.

"None of us like everybody, Yamin. But we have our friends and we like to make them happy. To our audiences we must give the news and hopefully a few moments of escape from difficult lives. Perhaps if they had more such escapes they would be kinder humans and then you would like them. At least that is how I think of it."

"So you don't like everybody?"

Studying the corner of the wall, the singer shook his head.

"But you smile at everyone, mostly."

The old singer frowned at something, but looked back at Yamin. "I prefer to give everyone the benefit of the doubt. I will like them and be kind until they prove me wrong. It is a most pleasant way to live my life and most of the time I have that kindness returned."

"You do?"

"I do indeed."

"So you think that I should just act as if everyone is good and be surprised when someone does something evil?"

Chuckling, the old singer patted Yamin's knee. "Not at all. Evil is out there—but we cannot live our lives always in fear of it. I would curl into a little ball and be afraid to move if I let the fear of evil take over. If I did, it would mean that evil has won, but it would have stolen the kindness from me and replaced it with fear. No, we have to live our lives with kindness and when evil happens, be saddened that it has consumed another life."

Yamin thought about it. He *had* been saddened when they discovered the culprit in their first mystery. In their second, he had forgotten to be sad and he supposed he had misunderstood when the old singer had been so upset.

"I think I understand. I can't look at all humans as the same. They are as different as Princess Minthamee is from me." He sighed and glanced sideways at the singer's kind old eyes. "No one here wants to do me ill. They are just as imprisoned by traditions as I am. I have to be patient." He looked down at his hands. "I don't think yoke thei are very patient creatures, singer."

The old man guffawed and Yamin leapt to his feet and danced a little jig. It felt good to dance again. He stuck out his tongue and then stopped. "Perhaps my problem is that yoke thei are not meant to have such human emotions."

"Perhaps it is more that each yoke thei is meant to feel only one emotion and you feel them all—or at least more of them than your brethren."

"You mean I can do things that they can't? Beyond investigating, of course."

The old singer nodded, but then leaned in close. "But don't tell them that I told you. It will hurt their feelings."

And Yamin knew it was true. Would they be jealous if they knew? Jealous like the young monks had been jealous of Hlaing Htay and Lwin Kwye?

A shiver ran up his back at the thought. He did not want to think about that possibility at all!

"What were you frowning at, Singer?"

"Frowning?"

Yamin rolled his eyes. These humans couldn't remember what they did from one minute to the next. "You were looking at the wall."

"Aah!" The singer nodded. "I was looking there. See? Those marks."

It looked like a stone wall. Yes, the stones were set tightly together—masonry to be admired—but was still just a wall. He leaned in closer to humor the singer.

There *were* marks in the niche. In the moonlight there were pits across the smooth stone. He stepped up close and sniffed, catching a whiff of human fingers.

"Someone was here. I can smell him on the stone."

The singer stood over him and ran his hand over the section of the wall. "It's as if someone has removed something from here and wanted to disguise that fact." He frowned.

"What is the problem, Singer? Perhaps there was an image no one liked."

Stepping back, the singer sighed. "A nat image, perhaps. The king would have them all removed." He shook his head. "It will be a sad thing to see only empty spaces. Min Mahagiri will be most upset." He turned back to Yamin. "But that is not my major concern. It is you, my fine fellow. How can I help you?"

The question was a surprise because it had always seemed that he was the one helping the singer, never the other way around. If he was the leader of their investigative team, then that certainly changed things. And it showed that the singer had use for him— and confidence. This was a murder mystery, after all.

In order to be commanding, he swallowed back the lump that had suddenly appeared in is throat. "Well," he said, hands on his hips. "I suppose we should discuss what to do next in our investigation. The troupe sent someone out to look for Lwin Kwye. Has anyone found him?"

He thought a moment, not waiting for an answer. As leader he supposed that it was proper that he not keep secrets from his partner. "And at the family home, did you see the man by the pillar?"

He looked up at the singer, waiting.

"I did not," the old singer said. "But I believe you that someone was there, for I saw the movement. What did you see?"

Yamin plopped down on the ground cross-legged again and scratched the base of his ponytail. Too bad for Zeya if he mussed his hair.

"He was in shadow, so it was hard to see his face, but he was broad of shoulder and broad of chest. Like one of those hug jars on the ox-drawn wagons."

"Barrel-chested you mean."

Yamin glanced up. "That would describe him. A barrel with legs." But what else was there? What color were his paso or his turban? All he remembered was gray. What was wrong with him? If he was in charge, surely he would remember more than that. "He had angry eyes. They were staring at us. Angry and hungry, I think. Like a tiger in human clothes." He shivered. "I would not like to meet him alone on a road."

The singer bent down to him. "Are you certain, Yamin? Are you sure he looked at us?"

Yamin nodded, remembering the chill he'd felt, as if all life and hope was withering away from him. He'd felt strength leaving him in the face of those glaring dark eyes. He could see them again and he was falling inside them, where he would be devoured. Those eyes had been looking at him.

Gasping, he tore himself from the memory and shuddered in the warm air. The voices of the puppet troupe and the apprentice singer's laughter were so normal it was a balm. He looked up at the old singer. "I am very sure. He might not have killed our young monk, but there is no kindness in him toward the likes of you and me."

"Interesting. And at the family home. Could it be misplaced anger that we found their son?"

"This anger was more than bone deep, Singer," Yamin said with a shake of his head.

"Then perhaps we need to find this man."

Yamin leapt up. If he was in charge, he would need to decide, and frankly he did not wish to actually meet such a man. "I think—I think we need to think on everything we've learned today and get some rest. You've walked very far. In the light of the morning, surely we will have new perspectives."

The singer's eyes widened in apparent surprise.

Yamin puffed up his chest, his hands on his hips. "What? What is it? Isn't that what you would have said?"

"Well, yes it is," the singer admitted.

"Good. Then I, for one, am going to bed." He left the old singer by the wall and headed for his basket. For once its confines were appealing. At times the world seemed dangerously big.

Chapter 8

The cool night wind placed gooseflesh across Aung's skin as he watched the little puppet cross the troupe's enclosure and clamber up the wicker trunks to slip under the lid of his own. For a moment he had the sense that Yamin had chosen to place himself in prison rather than face something. When describing the man he'd seen, a caul of darkness had seemed to cover Yamin's usually cheery features. Whatever was going on with the page, he was clearly troubled, and it was clearly this case that was doing it.

He sighed. The death of a child was never easy. It touched everyone around him in the community. And apparently young puppets as well. No—make that young-looking puppets. It was becoming more and more clear that, in Yamin, he was dealing with something frightfully capricious, but also very old indeed.

Struggling to make some sense of everything that had gone on, Aung shuffled to the fireside where Thura was telling some made-up tale about the foolish tiger and the naga, complete with different voices for each character. There was no question but that the lad would be a master singer one day. It was surprising that he did not chafe at the fact that Aung continued in the troupe, thus preventing Thura from assuming his rightful place. But then, the lad was still young and not all his decisions were good ones.

Thura leapt up at his approach and retrieved Aung's low, three-legged stool before resuming his story. Aung sank down and sighed at the comfort as U Myint passed him a still-warm, rolled banana leaf plucked from the fire's edge. Inside was the fragrance of rice turned crunchy and nut-flavored by its time in the fire. He thanked U Myint and dug in.

"There was no sign of the other boy," U Myint said, leaning in and speaking quietly. "I asked around, as did Thura. One of the oxcart drivers thought he saw the boy south of here crossing a field toward the river. He said he waved, but the boy did not respond. The driver thought the boy was carrying something."

At the news, all the fatigue that Min Mahagiri had lifted from Aung seemed to settle on his shoulders. What on earth was going on here? If Lwin Kwye was alive, why hadn't he returned to the monastery? More importantly, what would keep him away from both the monastery and his family, not to mention attending the funeral of his friend? Had the boy been heading to a hiding place when he was seen? Or had the oxcart driver been wrong? With their shaved heads and umber-colored robes, it would be easy to mistake one novice monk for another. Had it been another of the youngsters at the temple that the oxcart driver had seen?

Aung chewed on his questions while he ate his meal. The calming voices of the puppeteers and musicians flowed around him. Overhead the night sky was awash with stars that the moon could not erase, and moonlight glowed on the white stone of the pahto's corncob spire. Saya Lin settled onto the ground beside him.

"So how did the investigation go today? Have you discovered your murderer?"

"You know I have not," Aung said. "It's as if no one is a good suspect. There are possibilities, but none has a strong enough motive—at least as far as we can tell. That is very different than at Popa and Amarapura where there were too many suspects."

Saya Lin nodded. "It must be frustrating for that orderly mind of yours."

Aung smiled. "I fear my mind has become a hoarder of disconnected facts. They are strewn all around me and make no sense."

"I hope that you can at least find the sense you will need for our performance tomorrow evening. The merchant will have his child blessed and the nat spirits appeased."

Aung nodded. "I will do my best."

Saya Lin caught his wrist and squeezed. "You will be here and you will sing your best. We need this commission. Do you understand? There are rumors about us. We found the murder victim on Mount Popa. We found the young monk's body. There are whispers that perhaps what happened on Popa was our fault and we simply pointed the finger at another. There are questions about how we came to find the young man's body."

"Who is saying these things?"

Saya Lin shook his head. "I don't know who started the rumors, but it gets carried by the wind. I see the suspicion in people's eyes. Frankly, I'm surprised the merchant still wants us."

Aung looked to the moonlit corncob spire. "I'm thinking what better way to discredit an investigator than to cast suspicion upon him. Something evil is happening here. It affects even Yamin."

Saya Lin's eyes widened. "The page?"

"He is more sensitive than you think. The child's murder has sunk its teeth in him." He shook his head. "I think...I think tomorrow I must find those nuns."

§

The next day dawned with the promise of rain carried north on huge, towering thunder clouds painted red and black like an army. The river gulls flew before them like a vanguard on the brisk wind. Aung eyed the sky with distrust. This was the harbinger of a great storm. Farther south a solid bank of clouds covered the coast. Hopefully that was where the full brunt of the storm would be. As the rest of the troupe stirred around him with the groans of those who would prefer to sleep longer, Aung helped himself to rice left over from the last night's meal and then rose and headed for the curtain. He would find the two nuns if it took him all day.

"So you'll leave me here. Again. In a puppet's place, to do puppet things. Always kept in place by my strings."

Yamin's voice was more resigned than Aung had ever heard it. Certainly not the rollicking voice of the page he knew. He turned and found the little puppet seated on the edge of his basket. Leave him here as Aung should do, or do what his heart knew best suited the clever little page?

"You're awake. Good. I was going to find the two nuns."

"I can come?" Yamin's slumped shoulders straightened.

"In your pretend wood, of course."

The shoulders slumped again, but then the page brightened. "I'll still be able to see and gather evidence," he said with determination. "So you must carry me carefully so that I can see everything."

His bright voice was almost cheerful and Aung eyed him narrowly. There was a very good chance that he had just been played by the page.

"You planned to come all along, didn't you?" Aung asked as he settled Yamin in his arms.

"Wouldn't you, if it was your investigation?"

Aung didn't recall saying that Yamin was leading this investigation, but somewhere the page had come by that impression. Given the little one's state of mind these days, what harm would it do to allow the illusion?

"I suppose I would. It is a good thing you were ready or I might have left without you." He ducked through the curtain out into the warming morning.

The air was still cool but sunlight angled over the temple walls so that long golden columns illuminated the old items in the courtyard. A stone bench sat in the shadows of tree branches, a comfortable place for quiet contemplation. A large brass bell hung in a brick casement, the bell's weathered sides adorned with cast images of the Buddha's life. Once, the great bell might have been rung at the approach of mighty kings and lords, but for now the air carried only the doves' cooing and the buzz of cicadas waking in the sun.

The great entry to the temple gaped open, its sides carved with dancing images. Min Mahagiri, the greatest of the nats, guarded the temple entrance with his hammer. Long ago the ancient nats had pledged their support to Buddha and so they were still honored and worshipped at the temples—much to the king's displeasure.

Perhaps the king believed that the worship of the more ancient spirits stole prayer from Buddha and thus decreased the country's merit in the eyes of the gods. A foolish thought, but then Aung had come to understand that the king was trying to protect his country in every way he could.

Withering flowers rested at the foot of the nat image, so at least someone still honored them.

They headed out through the temple gate into the bright sunlight of early morning. He turned south, for the nuns must have escaped from Dhammayangyi temple southeastward otherwise the puppet troupe would have seen them. This early, the road was empty, for most families were either at their morning meal or in the fields that sustained them. Aung cast an uneasy eye on the clouds, but so far the great towers weren't gathering and the dark cloud bank in the distant south had not shifted northward.

"I was thinking about the nuns," Yamin said. "Could they have killed the young monk? They *did* run away."

"But only after they called us to the body. Why would they do that if they wanted to hide their responsibility? For that matter, would the boy have even been found if not for them? By the look of that temple, Hlaing Htay's body could have been left for weeks before anyone found it."

Yamin thought a moment. "His friend would have found him. Lwin Kwye. He'd have found him when he was climbing, I think."

"Very possible," Aung said. "Perhaps he did find his friend's body and that is why he is hidden—he fears for himself."

"Very possible," Yamin mimicked his voice and craned to grin up at him.

"Scamp!" Aung said. "I should make you walk."

Yamin glanced up at him hopefully, but Aung shook his head. He had to remember to be very careful about what he said.

It took most of the morning to reach the first village. It sat close by the river, next to a long, low temple. Aung poked his head inside and found a large reclining alabaster Buddha with the peaceful aspect of achieving nirvana. Used incense sticks poked up from a bowl of sand. Draped over the edge of the Buddha platform was a familiar marigold garland.

"The nuns have been here," Aung said. Though there was the possibility that others had prepared the garland.

They left the temple for the village.

It was a cluster of fifteen stilted dwellings, most unwalled and most situated around a central area that this morning served as a market area to people from beyond the village. Fishermen had their catch laid out on low stone slabs. Wicker cages held chickens. A woman sold eggs. Still another sold tomatoes, and another sold rags that looked like they were made of old longyi. In a village like this, nothing was wasted.

Carrying his now firmly-in-his-pretend-wood friend, Aung wandered among the shoppers. Clearly it was mostly a barter system. Few villagers had coin. He bought a lone tomato for his lunch and struck up a conversation with the female vendor who was curious about Yamin.

"That is one of the puppets, is it not? And a royal one, if these old eyes don't deceive me." She was an aging beauty, her lustrous hair now streaked with gray, the finest of lines now lacing her high cheekbones, eyes, and around her mouth.

"It is." Aung nodded. "I bring him with me to advertise that the troupe is here. There will be a pwe this night in the Ananda Pahto grounds to welcome a merchant's new child. I said that I would spread the word." It was as likely a story as anything.

The woman looked to the clouds that had momentarily blocked the sun. The air seemed heavy, as if the land was brooding.

"Not auspicious, but if the rain holds off, I may come." She nodded.

"The monsoons are upon us," Aung said, then casually changed the subject. "When we were coming into Pagan, our troupe happened upon a pair of nuns. I engaged in a lively conversation with Daw Ma Kyi and hoped to speak with her again. Do you happen to know where I might find her?"

"The Abbess? Of course I know her. She's usually here with her garlands for sale and produce from their gardens. Very good gardeners, those nuns. They always have extra to trade for their rice." She frowned. "I'm surprised she or Saw Nang aren't here."

"Can you tell me where I might find this household of nuns?"

She pointed southward. "Down that way. The next town, I think." Then she frowned. "But there was talk of Daw Ma Kyi joining her household to that of old Abbess Kyaw, who lives farther inland at a place with a small natural spring." She shook her head as she looked up at him. "I'm sorry. I can't be more help than that."

Aung thanked her and, carrying his tomato and Yamin, left the busy little market for the road southward.

It was very quiet, save for the sparrows twittering in the trees, the rush of the river over its mud and gravel banks, and wind gusts through the branches of the soapberry trees that grew beside the river. The road ran next to them and Yamin finally sat up and openly looked about, but he was far quieter than he usually was.

Aung had not gone far when the sound of approaching hoofbeats from behind turned him around. Trotting along the road came Harold Heath on his great gray horse. Beside him, on a donkey, rode a man clad in black with a wide-brimmed, low crowned hat.

"I say, there. It's Aung."

They rode up beside him and the two large men peered down. Harold Heath went bare-headed, his faded brown hair falling over his brow. The other man in black was a great stick of a man, with too-long arms and legs that seemed about to drag on the ground but for the way he rode with his feet tucked up in front of him.He wore dusty black trousers and shoes under a long black robe.

"I was just telling Father Blackmoor about you and your puppets, Aung. I see you have one of them here. Perhaps you could show Blackie, here, how they work. He's never seen a performance," Harold Heath said. He grinned his big-toothed smile.

Aung pulled Yamin a little closer, not liking that he was alone on the road with these men. Not liking that where there had been only one foreigner, now there were two, and Harold Heath's father to boot. Though Harold Heath had done nothing to rouse his suspicions, there was something about the man that Aung couldn't trust.

"I am a singer," Aung said.

Harold Heath and his father still looked at him expectantly.

"I do not dance the puppets," he said.

Harold Heath pouted. "Surely you can unwrap the strings and dance it around a little."

Aung was shocked. Yamin stiffened in his arms.

"Come now, man," the father said. "It's just a puppet."

Aung shook his head and backed a step. "It is not. He is yoke thei."

"See what I mean," Harold Heath said to his father. "It's like the damn things are their children."

The Father eyed Aung as if he was a creature he had never seen before. "Interesting."

Aung bowed his head. "Mingala ba—blessings upon you. I must be going."

He started on his way again, but the clopping of hooves said that the two men kept apace. They rode up on either side of him, leaving Aung feeling very small and unsafe. He gripped Yamin tighter and felt a small hand grip his shirt. The little page felt as threatened as he did. He squeezed the page in reassurance.

"So what are you doing out here so far from your troupe? Have you left them? After what I saw at that old temple, it can't be too safe for a man alone on this road. I say, would you be interested in selling that puppet? I could pay you a pretty sum of cash."

Aung glanced up at Harold Heath, both concerned and repulsed. Was the man threatening him for being out here alone? Was he going to try to take Yamin from him? "These puppets are not for sale."

"Then you're looking for the boy, aren't you?" said Harold Heath. "The whole damned countryside seems in a bit of an uproar about the whole thing. Everyone looking at strangers with suspicion."

Aung glanced up at the father and found the man's blue eyes—not quite as faded blue as those of Harold Heath—steady on him. It was like being held in the glare of a blue-eyed demon. He managed a weak smile and jerked his gaze away. What manner of men were these to see the world through such eyes. It was clear that they saw things differently than he did.

"You know, I've been thinking," Harold Heath said. "You asked me about the ruffians who were trying to steal your puppets. I said there were two of them, but there might have been more. I think I might have seen someone else around the back of the temple as I was passing by." He nodded at his father.

They reached the crossroad where Aung intended to turn farther into the dry plain of Pagan. "Where are you traveling, Harold Heath?"

The brown-haired man shrugged. "Oh, about. Out for a look at the temples again, you know. Odd sort of structures, don't you think? All that solid stone. Doesn't make sense, really, does it? Makes a man think of tombs and secret rooms. Just what were those old folks hiding do you think?"

Treasure hunters. Harold Heath was a treasure hunter and if he was, his father likely was as well.

"If there is treasure inside these temples, I have not heard. They are Buddhist temples. If there is treasure, it will be a Buddha hair or a bone, no more."

The two foreign men looked at each other. "Wouldn't that be something, father. An actual bone of the Buddha buried inside."

The father's jaw stiffened as if he did not approve of the thought.

"I must leave you here," Aung said. "I go to visit an old friend." He ducked from between the two horses and prayed they would not follow him. The absence of hoofbeats gradually loosened the tension in his spine and he checked over his shoulder. The two men still sat ahorse and apparently watching, though they seemed in deep discussion.

Aung hurried his step.

"Are they gone?" Yamin whispered.

"Behind us. I do not think they are following," Aung said.

"Thank you for keeping me safe, Singer." Yamin's voice was a whisper as if he still did not trust.

Aung didn't have the heart to tell the page that had the men tried to take Yamin, there was little Aung could have done about it.

He continued down the dusty road as the sun leaned into the afternoon and with the red dust rising at his feet to stain the bottom of his paso. Even the hem of his white Indian tunic had turned pink, and dust coated Yamin's usually white face. The trees were less frequent here, the fields looked barren. The dark spires rising from the dry landscape looked sullen as they brooded under the growing cloud cover.

Indeed, though the line of white cloud had entrenched southward, the number of towering, anvil-headed clouds streaming northward had increased. Now they seemed to jostle in the sky and low rumbles spoke of thunder, though the lightning was hidden in the clouds.

Aung hurried his pace. He needed to be back to the troupe by nightfall for the performance. He almost prayed it would rain, for the merchant might cancel the pwe as inauspicious and if the troupe wanted to be paid, Saya Lin would have to wait for astrologers to foretell another auspicious date for the blessing of the new son. If Saya Lin could be convinced to wait, it would mean that there would be more time for the investigation. There was no question but that they needed it.

Ahead rose a small copse of toddy palm trees, their fronds bristling at the top of their long trunks. To one side of them leaned five wood-sided, stilted huts that had faded to gray. As if it didn't quite belong to the ramshackle village, set off by itself stood one neat, walled enclosure, with a mango tree and three papaya trees sprouting from inside the enclosure to shade a larger wooden stilted house.

At Aung's approach to the main village, a mangy dog started barking and women left the shade under their houses. Men appeared like lice in the tops of the toddy palms, peering down at Aung as they took a break from collecting the sap from the palm fruit.

To one side of the houses stood a low structure that gave off the oversweet scent of toddy—the collected oversweet sap fermented into wine in only a few hours and into a strong liquor in just a day. Clay jugs were heaped around the distillery and an oxcart stood ready. The village would be carting their crop into Pagan market today.

Beside the toddy shack stood another small shed. A man in faded paso exited its door as a large, broad-shouldered man in breechclout and turban shimmied down the nearest palm to block Aung's way. The paso-clad man hurried over to them.

Aung set Yamin down and bowed, palms together at his chest as equals. The man copied his gesture, but his expression bore none of the open friendliness that Aung was used to from villagers. The man's gaze went to Yamin's wooden form and his jaw stiffened.

"I am Khin Htut, the headman of this village. What do you want?" He was thin, his ribs sticking out of his narrow chest, his arms and legs ropey with muscles. A muddy gray turban wrapped black hair turning to gray and his dark brown eyes had an odd ring of lighter yellow around the pupil.

"I am Aung of the royal puppet troupe. I seek the nuns Daw Ma Kyi and Saw Nang. I was told they live in a village in this direction."

The man glanced over his shoulder at the villagers gathered watching. Then he shook his head. "Not here. They live at a village an hour farther down the road."

The man turned to leave, which was entirely against Burmese etiquette. Usually villagers offered a meal to strangers—or at least laphet—the wonderful Burmese pickled tea—and water.

"Excuse me," Aung said. "I have walked a long way. May I trouble you for some water?"

Khin Htut looked over his shoulder at him and then nodded curtly to a woman. She rushed to bring Aung a clay cup of water as the headman watched. Aung drank his fill, for indeed the walk had been a dusty one. He thanked the woman and nodded his appreciation at Khin Htut. The man did nothing, but Aung felt his unfriendly gaze as he retrieved Yamin from the dust and started on his way.

Khin Htut motioned the gathered women back with a sweep of his hands and he returned to the shed. The big man retreated to the base of his tree.

"Not very friendly," Aung said to Yamin.

The little page's eyes flashed. Clearly there was something about the man.

No one else spoke as Aung circled around the village, past the walled enclosure. Beyond its gate he caught a glimpse of pink. He stopped. A pink nun's robe was thrown over a bush to dry in the afternoon sun.

The headman had lied.

He knocked on the gate and soon a pink-clad figure came scurrying and pulled the barrier open. Saw Nang's eyes widened in her round face as she recognized him and when she spotted Yamin she recoiled back a step.

"You! What are you doing here?" Then she remembered herself and placed her hands before her face and bowed.

Aung bowed his head to her. "Actually, I am looking for you and your abbess. You were supposed to join us in taking the young monk's body into Pagan town." He held up his hand when she started to protest that they had come, but he and his friends had already gone. "We sent searchers to the temple to look for you. You had already gone. And if you had tried to catch up to us, there would have been no problem, laden as we were with young Hlaing Htay's body. Now may I come in, or will you pretend like the village headman that you do not live here?"

Her gaze lowered. "I'm sorry. We do not like to be disturbed from our work and our studies." But she stepped to one side and bade him enter.

In the midst of the dry plains and next to the sad looking village, the enclosure was a paradise, with gardens thick with young vegetables and papaya at varying levels of ripeness hanging thickly on the spindly trunks of the trees. In the sunlight, lilies bloomed brilliant red and marigolds grew like a carpet in one corner. Someone had done washing this morning and more pink robes were spread to dry amongst the flowering plants.

In the center of it all, a tall stilted house stood with its door up a ten-step ladder. All was darkness beyond the doorway, save for bars of sunlight that cut through the house's slatted sides.

"Daw Ma Kyi is inside with the others," Saw Nang said.

She led the way through the garden and quickly climbed the ladder, leaving Aung to follow more slowly with Yamin. It was not an easy climb with the little one in his arms, but he managed with Yamin helping by holding on to his shirt and arm.

Inside it took a moment for Aung's eyes to adjust. Five nuns sat in lotus position on bamboo mats as Saw Nang joined them. Though Aung had thought Daw Ma Kyi was old, the others were ancient. Black eyes peered out of bald heads sunken to skulls. One was clearly blind with eyes the color of milk. As he stepped toward them they lifted their heads like beasts catching his scent.

He bowed, his hands close to his face, for these were venerable beings, even though they were women. "Thank you for seeing me, Daw Ma Kyi. Our interview was interrupted last time we met."

She blinked where she sat flanked by the older women, but said nothing.

Aung remained standing. "Why did you leave instead of joining us to take the body to Pagan as we had agreed?"

Daw Ma Kyi sighed and motioned him to sit. He did, joining them on the woven bamboo mat and setting Yamin on his lap. The old women's unrelenting gazes locked on the puppet.

"Why did you bring that with you?" Daw Ma Kyi enquired.

Aung shrugged. "A whim, I suppose. I thought it might encourage others to attend our performance tonight. Perhaps you would like to come to help bring luck to the child?"

She shook her head and pulled her gaze from Yamin. "It is as if he looks at me."

Aung smiled. "Perhaps he does. He is yoke thei. Spirits abide in them."

Three of the old nuns made sweeping motions with their hands as if he spouted nonsense. So these nuns did not believe in the old ways.

"Why did you leave?" Aung asked.

"Pardon?" Daw Ma Kyi said.

"Why did you leave the temple and not join us in taking the young monk into Pagan?"

"It was late and very far to come home. I considered that you would ensure the child's body was dealt with properly. As that was the case, I did not feel we were needed."

"Aah." Aung nodded, though her answer was too pat. He looked to young Saw Nang, who had joined the circle, for the young nun was likely to be less guarded. "Did you see anyone else near the temple?"

Saw Nang looked sharply up at him.

"There was no one," Daw Ma Kyi said.

"Is that also what you recall," he asked, holding Saw Nang with his gaze.

She met his gaze and then looked away. "Well... I thought perhaps, but clearly I was wrong."

Looking mildly at each of the nuns he considered. "That is very strange, because other witnesses report at least two ruffians and there was a foreigner on horseback as well. Think back. Are you sure you did not see them?"

Saw Nang's gaze fell away to the floor while the abbess held her with a glare. Outside the dimly lit house, the wind had picked up and gusts pressed their way through the wooden walls and floorboards. The storm was getting closer and the sunlight had dimmed. He needed to be leaving soon if he was to have any hope of escaping the storm and being back in time for the pwe.

"There was someone," The Daw Ma Kyi said. "We saw them from a distance. He was running to the north."

Which made no sense, given the rear of the temple had faced southeast. If whoever it was had truly been running north, they would have been seen by the puppet troupe as they waited for the nuns and the nuns would have had difficulty seeing whoever it was. Saw Nang kept her gaze averted to the ground as if afraid of what Aung might read in her gaze.

"And the rider. Did you see him?" He might as well check Harold Heath's claims while he was here.

"I saw no one else," Daw Ma Kyi said, but Saw Nang's head jerked as if she'd been poked.

Aung bowed his head. "I thank you for your efforts, though it is most troubling that we cannot find the young monk's killer. I suppose I have walked all this way for nothing."

But what he really needed was to get Saw Nang alone. The young nun was clearly not happy with the tale the abbess had told.

Aung climbed to his feet and retrieved Yamin. The little page was rigid, as if he truly was in his wood at the moment. Aung squeezed him in reassurance, bowed once more and went to the ladder. Saw Nang leapt up to guide him to the gate and presumably lock it behind him.

He clambered down the rickety ladder in the now-brisk wind. The sky had darkened and southward a black line of clouds sailed toward them, the main vanguard of the storm. "You'll need to take your laundry in, I think," he said as Saw Nang clambered down beside him and straightened her pink robes. The wind tugged at Aung's turban and white shirt.

She scanned the sky with him. "It will hold off yet for a few hours. It may even pass us by. Most of the rain seems to fall farther west along the river."

He frowned. "That's odd. You'd think you'd get the same rains here. It's not that far."

She shrugged and glanced up at the house, then led him toward the gate. She opened it and stopped him. "The rider was there. There were two of them. They looked as if they argued and then one rider headed north, while the other headed toward the temples along the river. Daw Ma Kyi made us hurry to get inside the temple before we were seen."

Aung nodded. "And the others? The ruffians?"

She shook her head, but her eyes were wide with urgency. "I cannot tell you anything." She shoved the gate toward him so that he stumbled back into the road.

Then she was gone. A soft "I'm sorry," floated out to him.

Chapter 9

The wind whipped the hem of the old singer's long tunic and shoved at his turban so that he was finally forced to cling to the headpiece with one hand. In the other he precariously balanced Yamin in a most unseemly manner.

Yamin finally sprang up on the singer's forearm and nearly spilled onto the road before he caught hold of the old singer's shirt. "Would you either carry me properly or put me down! I am not a sack of rice, you know!"

He glared up at the singer. It was odd, but he could swear that some of the lines had disappeared from around the singer's eyes, as if someone had smoothed the sand by the river to fill the old cracks. If his face was changing, did that mean he was changing inside, too? Yamin was no longer so certain about humans.

"You let those women lie to you." He went to fold his arms across his chest and almost fell again until he grabbed hold. The singer caught him to steady him, which was actually kind, but not enough to get Yamin to forgive him. "What kind of investigator are you?"

"I know they lied, Yamin."

That surprised Yamin a little. "But you just accepted what they said. Shouldn't we be asking them more and more questions until they trip themselves up?"

The old singer nodded thoughtfully as he plodded along the long straight road. The wind danced in the too-long hairs in his ears and in his heavy gray brows. "That would be one way to do it, but I fear it would not have ended to our benefit. Did you notice how the village headman lied to us, too? He did not want us to talk to the nuns anymore than Daw Ma Kyi wanted us to. Something is going on there. The question is what."

Yamin thought a moment. "Isn't the question whether what is going on has anything to do with the young monk's murder? The way you humans lie to, and treat, each other is really not something I care to know—except where it relates to my investigation." He hauled himself up onto the singer's shoulder and held to his collar against the wind.

Surprisingly, the singer didn't demand that he climb back down and pretend to be wood again.

"That is what I'm asking myself. What do you think, Yamin?"

"I think humans have far too many unattractive qualities. They lie. They kill. They treat each other poorly. Their young do it just as well as the older ones do." He ticked each of the faults off on his fingers. "Oh, and I forgot. They do foolish things like run away when they find a dead body." Something that had happened the last time the troupe had come across such a victim. "Do you think that's what happened to the young monk's friend?"

"Perhaps he did. Or perhaps he was somehow involved in the boy's death."

"Or he knows who killed the monk and fears it will happen to him," Yamin agreed.

"Or he's dead himself," Aung said softly.

"But how does that fit together with the nuns? And then there was that person in the young monk's village," Yamin said. "I wish I'd caught a better glimpse of him. All I recall is that he was very big—like that man in the nun's village—and he was not happy to see us at all."

The wind had picked up so that he had to hold on tight as dust lifted in sheets off of the dry plain and sifted down through the trees that lined the road. The old singer's lined face was covered in red dust. His shirt was, too, and Yamin had to slap his pantaloons to keep the blue cloth from turning purple. He looked over his shoulder at the sky. A misty pall obscured the plain southward and the wind grew wet.

"It's raining southward," he said. "You need to walk a little faster or we'll get wet. I really don't like my paint to get wet, singer. And Zeya always pulls my hair when he combs it out after its been washed. Can we please hurry back to the troupe?"

"Ahoy, there! Master Aung!" The voice came to them on the wind.

Yamin froze. Aung caught him and dragged him down into his arms as he spun around seeking the source of the voice.

Cantering up behind them out of the misty south came the giant on his great grey horse. He clattered up beside them. "I say, I think we're in for a sizeable storm."

"And where do you come from?" the singer asked.

"Me?" The giant's face took on feigned innocence that Yamin, for one, did not believe for a minute. "Why I was away southward going to see more temples, but

I got caught in the rain. I thought I'd hightail it across country to Pagan town, but then I caught sight of you and thought I might offer you a lift."

Apparently, giants lied, too, for this one's jacket and hair looked perfectly dry and the rain falling southward had looked most severe.

Of course, the singer would have caught that fact and would never agree to climb up on the horse.

The old singer looked behind them and then up at the horse. "A ride would be most appreciated. I need to get back to the puppet troupe for tonight's performance."

Nooo! Yamin wanted to yell.

The giant offered a hand down to the singer. "I'll hold your puppet, if you like."

Yamin froze. The old singer better not give him to the giant or he would definitely not be in his wood. He would bite the too-long, too-white fingers that would hold him.

Thankfully, the old singer shook his head. He adjusted his paso to form legs and caught the giant's hand. Suddenly it was as if they levitated up off the ground and the singer swung a leg over the gray horse's back. Astraddle, the singer slid in close behind the giant so that Yamin was squished between them, while the singer used one hand to catch the giant's waist.

Yamin glared, when the singer glanced down at him. The singer shook his head as if to admonish Yamin from doing anything—as if there was anything he could do from this vantage! He squirmed a little in the singer's arms so that he could see what was happening and where they went.

Then the horse started moving and the way the old singer bounced, Yamin thought his own teeth might come loose. How the singer held on, he couldn't fathom. Why the giant actually chose to travel in this uncomfortable fashion, he couldn't understand.

But then the giant didn't bounce about quite like the singer did. And there really was quite a marvelous view from this high off the ground. And apparently a horse could get from one place to another fairly quickly, for it seemed almost no time at all before the temples on the outskirts of Pagan town came into view. It had taken the old singer almost all day to travel the same distance. Hmm. Perhaps he would have to reevaluate his assessment. Perhaps giants weren't so stupid after all, if they used horses like this.

"You can drop us right here," the singer said, pointing at a cross road that led to the Ananda Pahto where the pwe would take place.

The giant rode past the crossroad. "I thought I'd take you into town."

"We need to get off now. The troupe is expecting us and we have a performance."

The giant reined in and the huge horse halted so suddenly that the old singer slid sideways toward the ground taking Yamin with him.

Yamin was sure they were going to take a tumble, but then a hand grabbed him. The singer fell and Yamin found himself hanging from too-white fingers and staring up into the too-blue, too-round eyes of the giant.

§

Aung landed in a heap in the dust, his left arm and shoulder twisting under him.

Yamin! He'd lost Yamin. He went to scramble up, but his left hip and knee seemed to refuse him. He lay next to the horse. He sought around him.

No Yamin.

"You looking for your little friend?" Harold Heath said.

Aung's gaze jerked up to him.

The smiling foreigner showed too many teeth. He had Yamin in his grip by the waist. He waggled the little page at him like a parent would waggle a doll at a child, and Aung was left with the feeling that he had utterly failed. Harold Heath could leave right now, and with his swift horse, Yamin would be lost to the troupe forever. A pulse of terror ran through him.

Aung tried to climb to his feet again, and again his left leg failed him.

Harold Heath's expression changed to one of concern. "I say. Are you hurt?"

"My leg..."

Harold Heath dismounted in one smooth flow, bringing Yamin with him. He set the little puppet on the ground and helped Aung to his feet and for a few hesitant and painful steps.

"Now I've gone and done it. There's no way you can walk home like this. You'll have to ride with me."

Aung shook his head. "Not to Pagan town." He gathered the precious little page into his arms and eyed the foreigner. "We will travel on our own. Thank you for the ride home." He bowed and, limping, turned to go.

"But I can give you a lift!"

Aung waved him away.

"Really! I was just hoping we could talk—about these puppets of yours."

Head down and teeth gritted against the pain, Aung kept on going. The clop of hooves came from behind.

Finally, he turned to face down the much larger man. "If you wish to see the puppets, I suggest that you attend the pwe. You will see their magic there."

The bigger man frowned. He shook his head. "I'm sorry you fell. I didn't mean for it to happen. And I'm sorry I touched the puppet, but I was only trying to keep him from falling. They—they are special puppets, aren't they? I swear he was looking right back at me. Such eyes he has. The windows of the soul, they say. Have your puppets a soul?"

Aung backed away, horrified at how close Harold Heath was to guessing the truth. There was a reason no one but a puppeteer must handle a yoke thei.

"I'm sorry. I must go." He turned and hobbled as fast as his injured leg would allow down the road. With every step he expected Harold Heath's hand to fall on his shoulder and Yamin to be wrestled out of his grasp.

There was no way that he would endanger the little page again.

Chapter 10

The area inside the temple's walled enclosure was a bedlam of activity. Regardless of the threat of rain, the merchant was determined that the pwe would occur. In a country as dry as Pagan, it turned out the merchant chose to view the rain as a blessing that would fall on the new baby during his presentation to the nats. The old singer staggered into the puppet enclosure and collapsed, almost unable to talk. His face was as pale as Yamin had ever seen it and his hands were shaking as he set Yamin down.

The singer crouched down and, gently holding Yamin's shoulders, he looked into Yamin's eyes. "I, too, am a human fool. I should never have taken you. I should never have encouraged your involvement in these investigations. It will not happen again."

"What are you talking about! You expect me to just sit here? This is my investigation!" The bustling puppet troupe flooded around them, putting a special cloth awning above the stage in case of rain. The musicians, likewise, gathered extra longyi to string on poles above their instruments. The puppet master who now acted as troupe master was hurrying from here to there, directing the construction. He stopped beside them and the old singer stood.

"By the nats of hill and forest, it's good to see you back," the puppet master said. "I was beginning to construct shows that did not include Yamin and believe me, that wasn't good. I had Thura in a corner practicing the Ramayana tale as a last resort."

"There is no need, though he would have done very well," the old singer said as if Yamin wasn't even there. He was going to go off with the puppet master and get off without even answering Yamin!

The puppet master hurried away and Yamin grabbed the old singer's paso and tugged. "I'm not finished talking to you! This is my investigation. You said!"

The old singer closed his eyes and shook his head. "If I did, it was only through allowing you to consider yourself in charge and I was wrong to do so. This cannot continue," he said softly. "You dare not leave the troupe enclosure. That—that foreigner—he had you and there was nothing I could do! He could have taken you, Yamin. He was on a horse. There was no way that I could have caught up to him. You would have been gone."

It *had* been a most harrowing experience—one he had tried to firmly put out of his mind. The giant's touch had felt so strange—as if it had a different vibration. He could feel it still in the pit of his stomach and the small of his back and it seemed to spread until it threatened the grain of his yoke thei heart. He shivered and felt cold and alone.

Then he shook himself, for dwelling on the touch would not help anyone—least of all him—and it might help a murderer.

"Well, he didn't and I am here and able to fight to conduct my investigation." He put up his fists and bounced on the balls of his feet.

The old singer closed his eyes again. He shook his head. "Don't you understand? I don't want to do this, either, but Saya Lin has been right all along. We cannot afford to lose you and I nearly did."

"So this is about you, then. Your worry. Your feelings." He crossed his arms over his chest, choosing to forget the terror he'd felt, to make his point about being in charge. It was time to test whether he and the singer were truly equal. "Well I, for one, will not stop this investigation. There is something very wrong here and I intend to unmask a murderer."

He turned his back on the singer and marched off to be alone and think, only to have his apprentice puppeteer come rushing up to him.

"There you are! The performance is only a little time away and look at you!" Zeya, his jolly young puppeteer, didn't look so jolly at the moment. He looked full of rules and remonstrations that were clearly going to be boring and at Yamin's expense, but before he could duck away, the young puppeteer had Yamin up in his arms and rushed through the bedlam to the wicker trunks. He set Yamin down and produced a comb.

"Look at your hair. And your face. And your clothes!" Zeya's distress rose moment by moment along with his voice.

Yamin rolled his eyes as Zeya set down the comb and found a clean cloth. He rubbed at Yamin's face, scrubbing at difficult bits.

He beat at Yamin's clothing to get rid of the dust and threatened to make Yamin strip so he could do a better job of it. Then he untied the sequined strings that tied Yamin's hair kand began to swiftly brush Yamin's hair, then roughly twist it into ponytails again.

"Stop it," Yamin sputtered. "I am not your plaything. You've smeared my face. You've pummeled my body and now you're pulling my hair. Enough." He yanked away and his untethered hair fell into his face.

Well, perhaps it wasn't quite enough.

He parted the hair so he could look out at Zeya. "At least manage my hair more gently. Please?" He pasted a winning smile on his face and a smile bloomed on Zeya's face.

"Of course, Yamin. My apologies on being so rough." He half-bowed to Yamin and gently combed his hair into place, wrapping the base of each ponytail with the sequined ribbon so each ponytail bounced perfectly in place. "There. Not perfect, but surely acceptable. You will need a bath, though, Yamin. After the show you shall have one."

A bath! Yamin's eyes widened. Though the yoke thei bathed with their human puppeteers and though water was always good for roots and leaves, too much water could rot wood, and water was only fun when played in for little boys—and pages. Baths were far too serious a business, what with washing out all the nooks and crannies.

Before Yamin could register his protest, the master puppeteer called the puppeteers together and that left Yamin momentarily alone. He leapt down off his basket, because no matter what the singer said, this was his investigation and investigate he would. There had to be at least an hour until the performance. The musicians hadn't even tuned their instruments and usually at a pwe there were other performers who performed before the puppet troupe.

That had to leave massive amounts of time for investigation.

Overhead, the heavy clouds had brought an unseasonable twilight that verged toward darkness. That would provide him with cover to do a little digging. Casually, he edged to the curtain by the mark in the corner of the wall, then quickly ducked underneath.

He stood in a tiny pool of shadow confined to a small niche in the wall that had once held a statue. Odd that the statue wasn't there. They didn't usually simply get up and walk away... But then the singer had said the king wished nat effigies removed. Had this spot held a statue of Min Mahagiri? Yamin stood as tall as possible, thinking of the handsome king of the nats whom he had met at Mount Popa.

Beyond, torchlight lit up the temple enclosure, staining red the white walls of the pahto. The flames guttered in the rising wind.

Here and there vendors had set up braziers and their coal embers glowed and sparked as grease fell from the goat and pork they cooked. Others deep fried small minnows pressed into rounds. A group of village musicians, who must be from Pagan town, struck up a playful tune on the hne and drums, so Yamin's feet danced a little in the still dusty soil. Women were seated on longyi spread on the earth, with clay pots of rice for their children's dinner. Of course, their children were nowhere about—they were running with the other young ones like flocks of birds across the temple compound, chasing a wicker ball.

Yamin imitated their footwork with the ball, but then caught himself and sighed. It all looked so idyllic, but there was a murderer amongst these villagers and happy children. He had discovered that every one of them had the potential to kill in their heart.

He crept along the wall looking for faces he knew from his time pretending to be in his wood. There was one—he recognized a man he had seen at the dead boy's village. Surely it was surprising that the man would come to the pwe so soon after the boy had died? But then, he didn't really know how humans felt about such things. They were ridiculously complicated creatures. Giants, too, apparently.

A flash of umber made him check around. Some young monks rushed to join the kick-ball game, while behind them came none other than Master Nu. He studiously avoided the kiosks of meat, for the Sangha— the brotherhood of monks—abstained from eating meat or drinking intoxicants.

Hold on a moment.

Master Nu threaded through the growing crowd gathered around the local musicians and greeted someone on the far side of the temple grounds. Unlike the other people who laughed together in the temple grounds, Master Nu wasn't smiling and he continued to frown as he spoke to whomever he had met in the shadows.

Yamin glanced at the village musicians. They continued to play and a town girl danced in the mincing little steps of an apsara dancer, though of course the real apsara dancers performed only at the king's court. The crowd was gathering and though the clouds loosed a few raindrops to spatter on the ground, it seemed that the musicians and dancer would perform a while yet.

Glancing back at the curtained puppet troupe enclosure, he edged behind some overgrown grass in the direction that would take him to Master Nu. Thankfully, as the people continued to gather, the children had mostly taken their game of kickball beyond the walls.

From the tuft of overgrown grass, he edged sideways though an area where the torchlight had dispersed the shadows in a veil along the wall. He held his breath and paused after each tiny step in case someone saw him. If they did, hopefully he was just a half-seen stone image carved into the wall. But no one approached him. No one commented.

He heaved in a deep breath when he reached the next patch of shadows.

Then the singer's familiar voice reached him and he froze. What would they do to him if they found him?

§

Aung stepped beyond the curtains, already certain he knew what had happened. The damnable page had decided to continue his investigation regardless of the danger it posed. At the moment the rest of the troupe was in an uproar because Zeya had turned back to Yamin only to find the little puppet had disappeared. Zeya's alarm had brought the entire puppet troupe turning to Aung.

"I definitely told him to stay put!" he'd said—not that anyone had believed him. Even Thura had raised his brow and Saya Lin had turned a castigating frown on him. Together they searched the puppet enclosure, but Yamin was always easy to find in the puppet enclosure. In the past he'd always been the center of some prank at someone else's expense—most notably the Mintha. If he wasn't easily found, then he wasn't there at all.

No, after his conversation with the page, Aung had no question at all about where Yamin was. Out here in the growing dusk, the rain, and the mounting number of people. Aung could think of very few places less suitable.

The larger question was where Yamin would go. He was a determined little creature, of that Aung was certain. And given Yamin's concern about the investigation, there was no question but that he would be doing his best to gather evidence.

But gather evidence from whom and why?

Being small, he could spy on people very well, so who amongst the pwe attendees would warrant such attention? Aung scanned the shifting crowd, but the densely packed numbers around the Pagan town musicians meant that individuals were hard to distinguish. The merchant he recognized as the man who had spoken with Saya Lin stood near the gate into the temple courtyard. He greeted everyone who came, and the new arrivals dutifully entered the temple to make offering to Buddha on behalf of the merchant's infant, but not all were attentive to the ornately wrought spirit house that the merchant had had erected for the occasion.

It was a superb piece of woodwork, standing on a beautifully carved single pillar that stood about five feet high, with ornately carved roofs, walls, and lintels that exposed Min Mahagiri's seated effigy inside the golden wood structure. Even fifteen feet away where Aung stood, he could smell the sweetness of the carved sandalwood.

At its base, the earth was heaped with offerings to the king of the nats—the same spirit who had gifted Aung with a reprieve of age. Banana leaves were spread and heaped with rice. Tightly packed lotus blossoms in clay bowls of clear water would soon explode to magnificent lilies. Coconuts were set in clay bowls amid the rice and garlands of marigolds that hung from the spirt house's roofline.

As he watched, a man and woman skirted the offerings but added nothing of their own. The spirits would be incensed, in Aung's opinion. The merchant was taking a chance even having those people attend. Had he not thought of how he was garnering the spirits' attention by hosting the pwe as a means of asking for their blessings?

Momentarily setting aside his concern for Yamin, he crossed to the merchant.

"Good evening," he gave a small bow with his hands palms-together before his face in acknowledgement of the man's wealth. "I am Aung, the puppet singer. I noticed that some of your guests do not make offerings to the nats. Do you not think that is risky when seeking the nat's favor for your son?"

The merchant chuckled and bowed graciously. He had the round little belly of the prosperous man, and around his neck a gold chain held an amulet blessed for wealth, Aung would guess. The man's pristine white high-necked shirt made Aung feel shabby in his road-stained clothing but the man had a kindly face.

The merchant shook his head. "I am a man of the world, singer. I know what is what. I do this because it is tradition and because it will impress and infuriate my competition—not because I place importance in spirits. Fickle things all of them, if you ask me. Why do we need them if we have Buddha? If I gain merit, what can the spirits do to me?"

Aung swallowed back the bile that rose in his throat. This was no pwe—it was a—a show. A chance to show off that this man could afford the royal puppet troupe to bless his son—nothing more. He swallowed back his horror and nodded.

"A modern man, indeed," he said. "Are there many here in Pagan town who are so modern?" And so in keeping with the king's edicts to cease propitiating the nats.

The merchant shrugged. "Not so many. Most of the villagers still believe in nats of one sort or another. A nat that keeps a spring bringing water. A nat that helps the rice field. A nat to keep your household safe." He shook his head and looked conspiratorially at Aung as if he expected a member of a troupe patronized by the king to share the king's beliefs. "A lot of nonsense, if you ask me. Spirits have nothing to do with good fortune. Unless, of course, you trade on that belief." He looked down his nose at Aung.

Is that all the troupe was to people like this man? Traders in superstition? Charlatans?

The arrival of more guests turned the merchant away from Aung, leaving him with a chest tight with worry. Had the king's edict caused this rift in belief, or had it always been? If more people stopped believing, what would happen to the country? Didn't people understand the power of the nats?

A light touch on his arm turned him around. It was the woman who ran the restaurant they had first stopped at when they arrived in Pagan with the body.

"Htet Hla! It is a pleasure to see you again." He bowed with hands pressed together at his chest. She matched his gesture, her dark eyes shining, and he was struck again by the beauty that underlay the net of age lines on her face. This late in the day, the usual smears of white thannaka paste were absent from her cheeks because she needed no protection from the sun.

Her smile beamed up at him. "I thought it was you. It is good to see you as well. Your troupe will perform tonight, I hear."

He bowed his head. "That is so. In an hour or so. Hopefully the rain will hold off."

Together they scanned the sky.

Htet Hla shook her head. "Too bad the pwe is not held in some of the villages south of here. Some of them rarely get rain."

"Truly? Pagan plain is dry, but the monsoons eventually come," he said.

"That is so." Htet Hla nodded. "But there are places where the people no longer propitiate the nats. They say that is why the rains never come there."

More villagers swirled around them and the torchlight guttered and dimmed as if something took displeasure in her words. A flash of light illuminated the clouds from within and from them came a low rumble.

"So they are like our host: they don't believe in the nats anymore."

Htet Hla shook her head. "The same and yet not. Our host simply does not believe in them, but he is a good Buddhist and makes fine offerings to the temple. Others are less good—or so I hear."

He considered what she was telling him. It might have nothing to do with the murder, but anything that would help him to understand Pagan might help him understand who would have motive for murder.

Watching her closely, he posed his next question. "Do you know the nun, Daw Ma Kyi?"

A flicker of surprise crossed her face. "Of course. Who does not? She is the Abbess out at Khin Htut's village. She had her own place in Pagan village but old Abbess Kyaw became ill and the other nuns with Abbess Kyaw were so old that Daw Ma Kyi and one or two other young nuns went out there to care for them. It might have been for a compassionate reason, but it was not a good move. She has lost a number of her younger nuns to other communities." Her mouth hardened and she shook her head.

Aung stayed silent, for he had long learned that others were uncomfortable with silence and that discomfort led to them disclosing more than they might otherwise.

"From a thriving community in Pagan, she now lives hand-to-mouth in a parched village."

By the shake of her head, he was fairly certain that Khin Htut's village was one of the disbelievers' villages.

"They are fortunate that there is a spring in the village. It allows the toddy to grow and the people to live there. I am surprised the nat of the spring has not left the place and let the spring run dry." She shook her head.

"So you still believe."

She looked up at him and the torches caught in her eyes as if a flame burned deep within. "Always," she said. "I helped my father make offerings when I was barely walking. I have bowed to the shrines ever since. I am a Buddhist, but the nats bow to Buddha. Why shouldn't I continue to believe in them? My business goes well. My children are happily married with children of their own. I may have lost my husband to brigands a year ago, but my life has been a full one."

It was a pleasure to meet someone who had such strong beliefs and who carried her smiling *bhammasan chin*—her calm Burmeseness—like a cloak around her.

"My condolences on the loss of your husband," he said.

"Thank you," she said. "It was difficult, but it was a test, was it not? Just as all life is a test. The question we must all ask ourselves is how we will pass it. Yes, I could have mired myself in a sea of tears, but what help would that be to myself or anyone? I prefer to pray for my husband's good rebirth and to carry on living. I started my restaurant then, to keep myself busy."

She smiled and it was a good smile, her small white teeth catching the light.

"The hardest part was it was all so sudden," she said as they walked among the milling crowd. "He had gone out to our field near Dhammayangyi Pahto and never came back. I went to find him and there he was, strangled. The ox and plow were still standing waiting for his direction." She closed her eyes at the old painful memory and a single tear squeezed from under her eyelid—until she scrubbed it off and started walking more briskly through the crowd. "I am sorry. The death of Hlaing Htay brought it all back. That is why I was so shocked when you arrived with his body and told me where he had been found."

"He must have loved you very much," he said, keeping up with her.

She glanced at him. "How would you know?"

He smiled and shrugged. "Because a man so well-loved should always love more in return or else he is a fool."

"My husband was no fool," she said with a grateful smile.

"Did they ever find who killed him?" For news of this earlier death was troubling. Dhammayangyi Pahto was where the young monk's body had been found.

Htet Hla shook her head. "No one lives out there. There was no one to see and no one to suspect other than brigands. It would have taken a very strong man to kill my Ye Tun."

They circulated through the crowd in silence and Aung scanned near the walls and in the shadows for Yamin. Please let the little scamp have thought better of being out in this crowd. Please let him have returned to the troupe's enclosure. But knowing Yamin, there was little chance that would have happened. He needed to keep looking for him, but there was something about the information Htet Hla was giving him. It *meant* something. He was sure of it.

The music had turned from lively to wild and over the tops of the crowd's heads he could see the arms of the girl as she whirled around.

Htet Hla shook her head. "They'll take their pleasure watching the girl, but they won't make an offering or believe in the spirit that takes her."

Aung looked at his companion in surprise. "The girl is a spirit wife?"

"They come upon her—have since she was a child—but she has chosen to marry and stay home with her husband and child. Our host must have paid her very well to dance here tonight."

A nat wife. That explained the electric feel of the air and the sense that something other swirled around them in the wind. For some reason the nat wife's presence surprised him.

"There must be many people who disapprove of her."

"Not too many," Htet Hla said as she waved to a friend seated close by the newly lit bonfire in the center of the courtyard with a younger woman and children—a daughter and grandchildren, most likely. "She lives quietly and does not make a show of her other—skills. She gives many hours to sweeping temple courtyards."

Aung frowned. It did not make sense. "But you said that there were many disbelievers here."

Htet Hla trained her full attention on him. "Yes, but so close to Mount Popa it is more greed that fuels their disbelief. I have heard that with the foreigners coming to the coast, there is an interest in things that are old. Some have taken it upon themselves to fuel this interest."

"The empty niches in the walls. The missing Jataka stones."

Htet Hla sighed and shook her head. "It is poorly done. It turns our people into no more than scavengers, ravaging their sacred places—and for what? A few pieces of silver? And when the silver is spent, what are you left with?" She tsk-tsked and looked past him. "These foreigners. I do not think I like them. Too big, too pale, and they speak a garbled language. I think this one comes for you."

Aung turned. The torchlight by the temple gate caught on the faded brown of Harold Heath's hair and turned his pale face ruddy as he scanned the crowd. It was as if the people parted before him and the open path led right for Aung. Then the darkness parted behind Harold Heath and his Father Blackmoor stepped up beside him.

Harold Heath led the way across the temple courtyard to Aung. "Aung, old man! I thought I'd take you up on your invitation. You remember Father Blackmoor. I convinced him that as men of science we should see these puppets of yours in action."

Harold Heath's open face was almost eager. Beside him Father Blackmoor's narrow face spilt in a smile.

"I've heard stories of the puppets. They are important to some people," Father Blackmoor said.

"And these are royal puppets, old son," Harold Heath said. "I'd think they'd be better than most. Whatd'you say, Aung? Are they truly better?"

Aung had followed the banter of the two men. He bowed his head under the first light rain. "So it is said. You will have to tell me after you have seen the performance." He glanced toward the stage. The torchlight beyond their curtained enclosure showed hurried movements. Thura stepped outside the curtain and caught Aung's eye. The apprentice singer shook his head.

Yamin was still missing and these men were about.

Belly tight with worry, he turned back to excuse himself from the two foreigners, but Harold Heath caught his arm. "Why don't you indulge us and show us around before your show?"

It was the farthest thing from what he wanted, but he had caused this problem by inviting Harold Heath. The least he could do was show the foreigners around and get them seated—as far from possibly seeing Yamin as he could arrange. Then he would finish his search.

Sighing, Aung went.

Chapter 11

Yamin pressed himself into the rough niche in the wall. The stone was rough and dug into his back. A slight rain patted his face. His toes and fingers ached from holding himself in place, but the good thing was that no one seemed to notice he was here. After all, a dancing figure was supposed to be in this niche. Where it had gone, he didn't know. Perhaps it didn't like its lot in life any more than he liked his. Perhaps it would like to take his place. A chortle fizzled out in his throat. It would be amusing to see the puppeteer's faces when they opened his trunk and found a figure of stone.

Beyond his meager hiding place, the courtyard teemed with so many humans. Men and women talking. Mothers with their children settled on blankets now that the hour was running late. A storyteller had spread his cloth on the far side of the temple courtyard, beyond the large bell near the temple entrance, and a crowd had gathered to hear his tales.

Which meant that the music and dance would be ending soon and the people would drift away. That would leave him exposed to the old singer's search, for if anyone knew he would be out here it was the singer. The trouble was that Yamin still hadn't managed to catch up to Master Nu. Between the press of people and too much torchlight, even his ability to go unnoticed had been sorely tested. And now the people were shifting again.

A flash of light-drinking umber caught his eye. There! There was his quarry, standing with two other men.

He eased down from his hiding place and scurried along the base of the wall trying to get close enough to hear their conversation, but when he reached the area of the wall closest to them, the noise was too great for him to hear. Leave the wall?

There was a stone bench under the trees in the courtyard. If he could get through the tangle of legs, the bench might just be close enough to hear what Master Nu said. He watched his timing, planning a route through the longyi- and paso-covered legs. Taking a deep breath as if he was diving in deep water, he dodged between the people.

When he reached the bench, he dove underneath and lay on his back simply breathing in relief. He'd nearly been stepped on or kicked too many times. His only saving grace had been that he was fast—faster than unwary human feet, at least.

And there it was. A simple yoke thei page had outsmarted all those humans. He sat up feeling satisfied with himself and peeked out from under the bench.

Wonder of wonders, the people had shifted again and this time umber robes hung like a curtain directly in front of him. He reached out and touched their thin cotton in disbelief. It was true. Master Nu was here with his friends and one of the friends was talking.

"We've looked everywhere and he's not to be found. Gone to ground, that one."

"Or he's left town. He always was a sneaky child. Liked to spy on his betters just like his cousin. If he's gone, we're well rid of him."

"He's a child," said Master Nu's kindly voice. "Where would he go? No, I think he's hiding somewhere near."

They had to be talking about Lwin Kwye, the missing boy! Yamin strained to listen, but a booming voice cut through the pwe's clamor.

Yamin jerked back under the bench. It couldn't be and yet it was! The giant was here and for the first time since he'd left the puppet enclosure he felt a tremor of fear. He didn't like the giant. He liked it less that the man had held him and he liked it even less than that, that a part of him still quivered at that touch. It was like all his nerves were jangled. All his thoughts, too.

What was he doing out here? What had been so interesting to listen to?

He shivered, not sure of the answers, but the glimpse of a dusty foot poking from under the umber hem reminded him and he crawled to the edge of the bench again.

"...he doing here?" one of Master Nu's friends said. "We were never to meet in public!"

Yamin sat up and bumped his head on the bench. One of his ponytails got scrunched and he was pretty certain he was going to have a goose egg on his skull. Zeya would not be pleased, but too bad for him. The investigator was just doing his job.

He leaned out again, but Master Nu's robes blocked the view. He followed the booming voice to peer out from the other side of the bench and there, along with the giant, came the giant's father and the old singer. Yamin's lips pressed together. The giant was surely a suspect and the darn singer was stealing Yamin's investigation! It wasn't fair!

He threw himself down beneath the bench just as Master Nu shifted position. While one of his companions was still blocked from view, the other was revealed as none other than the large breechclout-wearing man who had been up a tree in the nun's village. Yamin eyed the fellow who was bathed in shadows and then gasped. It was him—the half-seen figure from the dead boy's funeral! In the full sunlight Yamin hadn't recognized him at the nun's village.

But that made no sense. Why would such a man be involved with the monk—or with the young monks, come to that? What had he been doing at the funeral and why had he looked so fiercely at the old singer and himself? He hadn't seemed so fierce at the nun's village. Indeed, he'd not said a word, even if his body language had been threatening.

But why would he do that? Was he protecting something in the village? Was he afraid of the singer talking to the nuns? But they hadn't told the old singer anything—in fact they had been particularly unhelpful—except for the last words of the young nun. She'd said that she had seen the giant on his horse near the temple where the young monk was found.

"They are coming this way. We should not be together," said the third, unseen, man.

The man shifted back from the others, but though Yamin craned to see him, taking a chance and leaning out from under the bench farther than he safely should, the darkness once more protected the man's identity. There were too many intervening bodies and the singer and the giant were almost here.

He had two choices—stay and spy on the singer, which would be most satisfying—or follow the unidentified man. If he stayed he'd learn what the old singer said, but that didn't mean he'd learn anything new, and he already knew more than the singer.

He ducked back under the bench and out from the other side, trying to keep the other man in sight. He was just one more male figure clad in a plaid paso, and would be so easy to lose. He didn't dare run for the wall—if he did, he'd lose the man for sure.

There was no help for it. Surely in the dim torchlight and the crowd no one could see their feet clearly. He had to take a chance.

He darted out into the sea of legs, praying no one, including the singer, would see him.

§

A Death in Passing

Aung caught the brief flash of movement as he bowed his head in greeting to the venerable monk. There was a small tossed head, the glitter of sequins and small pearls, and a small disappearing bare foot, lost amongst the intervening sweep of paso and longyi hems. He nearly dove after the damnable little scamp. What in Buddha's name was the little page doing? Didn't he know the danger he was in? Or were matters dire enough the page thought the risk acceptable?

"Master Aung, so you and your puppets will perform. I'd thought you were intent on heading south to Yangoon."

Aung swung back to Master Nu. He didn't recall telling the monk those things, but then news travels fast in a place as small as Pagan.

He shrugged. "Your merchant took our presence as a sign it was time to seek the nats' blessing for his child. Yangoon will still be there when we arrive."

The monk nodded sagely. "Still, it is troublesome when one's plans are delayed."

Aung kept a straight face, but what was this? A monk did not present such opinions. A true teacher would speak of how all sense of time and all frustrations were simply the churning of one's own mind in its never-ending search for pleasure and satisfaction. A teacher would remind that Buddha taught that all such frustrations simply pass away, like dust before the wind.

Aung eyed Master Nu and his companion with new consideration. The big man Aung had last seen in a breechclout in the nun's village stood stiffly in his blue longyi beside the monk. His broad shoulders strained the frayed seams of his plain white shirt and a tightly coiled turban perched on his head.

Aung nodded in his direction. "I believe we have met, but were not introduced. I am Aung Aung of the puppet troupe. I had not thought to see you here." He waited politely for the monk to introduce them or the man to introduce himself.

The man shrugged, not offering his name. "A man works when he has to, to feed his family, but the chance to see your puppets was too good an opportunity."

Aung bowed his head slightly as if in thanks for a compliment. "Did Khin Htut come with you? Or the nuns?" Perhaps he could try his luck with Daw Ma Kyi or Saw Nang again.

"I came alone." The man bit off each word as if it betrayed him. "There can be poor influences at festivals like this. Besides, given the death and the disappearance, it seemed best not to leave our children alone at home."

Aung nodded again and sighed. "Perhaps you are right. It is most troubling." He turned back to Master Nu. "Has there been any word on the missing child?"

Master Nu's shoulders slumped as he shook his head. "There's been no word. No sightings at all. It is as if the child disappeared into thin air."

Aung considered. Was it possible that Master Nu hadn't heard about the sighting that U Myint had reported?

"One of our puppeteers reported a sighting near the river," Aung said, studying the two men for their reaction.

There was the barest of flickers in the villager's gaze. Master Nu's expression of concern didn't change.

"I believe we followed up on that report. There was nothing to it," Master Nu said. "Truly the child has disappeared. I fear his body may never be found." He closed his eyes, apparently in brief prayer.

Aung glanced at Harold Heath beside him, once more seeking any recognition of the two Burmese men. "We discuss the missing child. Have you met Master Nu of Pagan monastery? This is Harold Heath and his Father Blackmoor." Was that a flicker of recognition in Master Nu's gaze?

The two foreigners looked to the monk with interest and Harold Heath provided a reasonable bow with palms together—so the foreigner was learning to be socially acceptable. That was something.

"It is a pleasure to meet you, sir," Harold Heath said in stilted Burmese. Father Blackmoor nodded but made no other show of greeting.

And by the foreigners' expressions it was possible that they hadn't met before—or else Harold Heath was an actor of a quality Aung had not seen before. Was everything about the man an act, a façade? What lay underneath those pale eyes and too-sharp features? Not for the first time he wondered just why Harold Heath had not robbed him of Yamin. He could have killed Aung and left his body and taken what he wanted. Did that mean the man hadn't been involved in Hlaing Htay's death even though there was evidence pointing at him?

Perhaps Aung had been imagining he'd seen something in Master Nu's gaze.

Aung looked back to the milling crowd that now gravitated toward the storyteller, hoping for another glimpse of Yamin.

Nothing.

The village musicians had stopped and the dancer had returned to her role as a housewife. The storyteller's voice rose and fell above the murmur of the crowd and the patter of the rain on the surrounding htaung trees. Indeed, the rain was increasing and a deluge would not help Yamin's appearance. Saya Lin was already likely mad with worry and furiously determined that Aung had somehow put the idea to disappear in the little page's head. Did he dare leave Master Nu and the others together in order to retrieve Yamin? He had not much choice.

He turned back to his companions. "I must apologize, but the troupe's performance grows near and there is something I must do."

He excused himself and set off in the direction he'd seen Yamin disappear, but kept an eye on the men he had left behind. They were backlit by the bonfire and appeared to be in conversation, the Father Blackmoor offering up translation skills Aung had been unaware of.

Pushing through the crowd, he was surprised that the direction the page had gone did not head back toward the safety of the wall. Instead, Yamin appeared to be have headed toward the Ananda Temple's entrance.

Perhaps it was the trees that stood by the opening provided shadows to hide in or, perhaps, shelter from the rain. That could be all Yamin had been seeking.

That and eluding capture by Aung. The little scamp had likely seen Aung and purposely run. From what had been a team that had successfully investigated two crimes, something had clearly eroded their relationship. Aung couldn't pinpoint what it might be.

Worrying about the answer, he shoved through the last people to reach the trees. The crowd had thinned here and birds disturbed by the pwe rustled in the leaves above. The sweet scent of incense wafted out the gaping door to the temple.

Had Yamin gone inside to hide?

Aung started for the entrance, but stopped at the sound of stone cracking. People rarely visited these old temples so late at night. Those who did brought offerings of food and flowers to lay at the feet of the oversized Buddha figures and the nat images that accompanied them. There was no reason for such a sound.

Creeping forward, he reached the temple entrance. There was no sign of Yamin, but, like at Dhammayangyi temple, looming just within the temple entry was a huge, seated, alabaster Buddha figure, its white cheeks turned ruddy by the firelight. Aung's eyes adjusted enough to see through the shadows to the offerings of rice and bananas heaped upon banana leaves at the Buddha's feet earlier in the day, and the stubs of the old incense he'd smelled.

Also like Dhammayangyi, Ananda was built with a huge square base that was apparently tunneled through by tall ambulatories that led left and right from the entrance. To the right, the ambulatory was only darkness, but to the left, a candle's glow illuminated the pale corridor walls and a small alcove far down the long hallway. A figure knelt there brandishing a chisel on the wall.

Here was the person responsible for the stolen images he'd noticed on Pagan temples.

But before he could even fathom what this might mean, between Aung and the kneeling person a shift of shadows provided a brief glimpse of what could be small double ponytails. Then the apparition was gone, disappeared into shadows.

§

The candlelight flickered in the long ambulatory of the huge pahto, the place otherwise so dark and huge that to Yamin it felt like he had followed a demon into the depth of a mountain. Cool air scurried across the cold stone floor and stuck to the wall like the shadows he crept through. Behind him, the huge doorway into the temple's first level allowed in the fire and torchlight of the pwe. He could not afford to be silhouetted against that glow.

The air smelled of dust and old incense and shadows, and the breeze along the ceiling sounded like whispers. Perhaps it was human ghosts—or hungry ones—waiting to see what the man ahead was doing.

Or perhaps it was only the wind.

Either way, occasionally dust flaked down off the ceiling and something—an animal, perhaps—sent a stone rattling and the man he had followed looked up, checking both ways down the ambulatory as if afraid of being spotted.

It was the kind of action one equated with a thief. Yamin pressed his lips together. Was it a large leap from thief to killer? He wasn't sure, but greed was a motive, or so the old singer said.

For a moment he missed his co-investigator, for if there were two of them, it would be much easier to deal with this human.

The fellow—a youth he recognized from the dead boy's village—was crouched beside an alcove and from Yamin's position it looked like the alcove contained a dancing figure. A nat effigy, most likely, for old temples were often homes to both Buddha and the nats that had bowed their heads before Buddha's greater truth. Now they helped guard the Buddha's abodes.

The youth pulled something from a bag he had over his shoulder and a soft clang echoed down the length of the ambulatory. The youth checked over his shoulder again in a most suspicious manner. Clearly, he was about to do something that was not allowed.

He set a metal spike against the pahto's wall and began to chisel a line around the dancing figure.

Yamin fell back in shock. Was the human destroying the nat? Or stealing the figure?

Either way, it was a heinous act and must be stopped. He tapped his small toes in the dusty floor, then caught himself for fear the motion would be seen.

He was too small to just walk up to the human. Besides, the old singer had been adamant that he should not be seen, and given the way this human was treating an effigy of a nat, it was pretty likely that the old singer was right—this time.

Go for help?

By the time he made it back to the puppet enclosure and convinced one of the puppeteers that something needed to be done, it was highly likely that the culprit would be gone—if the puppet master or any of the others would listen to him at all, consumed as they were with tonight's performance.

So that wasn't an option and that meant that he needed to do something himself. He needed to somehow convince this human to stop what he was doing, but that would take more than a yoke thei's convincing. A message from Min Mahagiri himself? Hmm.

The pahto wall was rough from the fall of decorative plaster over the years. It he could climb up and perhaps find a niche above, he could pretend to be the king of nats. Surely Min Mahagiri would forgive him, given the worthy cause.

He slid farther along the wall, searching for hand and toe holds and finally found a likely spot where two sections of wall were joined together by a stone arch. He leapt as high as he could and silently started climbing, checking over his shoulder at the man.

He reached the high, arched ceiling, but in this location a smooth expanse of ceiling painted with scenes from Buddha's life met the wall. There were no more finger and toe holds and no niches either. Whatever he was going to do, he was either going to do it from here or not do it all.

He sucked in a deep breath and aimed his voice at the ceiling. It should reverberate nicely from there—he hoped. And hopefully scare the human.

"I see you, man! You will pay for defiling my temple!"

Hurrah! His voice boomed and echoed nicely before rolling across the floor, even if it did cause dust to cascade down from the ceiling. It got in his eyes and clogged his chest so he wanted to cough. The man leapt up and turned toward the door. He stopped and Yamin, mouth open and ready for further tirade, followed his gaze toward the temple entrance.

Yamin froze. A singular silhouette from a singular human stood not far below. Just how the old singer had come so close without Yamin hearing, he wasn't sure. Perhaps it was that he'd been so intent on the thief by the wall.

The thief leapt for the singer as if he thought the old singer had spoken. The singer was shoved into the wall, the young man's hands at his throat. He slammed the old singer's head against the stone again and again and the singer's mouth was open, working like a fish in a boat!

He couldn't breathe! The thief was killing him just as he'd killed the little monk! Those hands were strong enough they could kill anyone and without the old singer, the puppeteers would never ever let him investigate! They'd likely keep him locked in his wicker basket and Yamin would have lost his very best friend in the world—his co-investigator!

He could not lose his friend!

He leapt, throwing himself like a bat, his vest spread wide to catch the air. He slammed into the thief's shoulders and knocked him away from the singer, but then horrible hard fingers grasped his shoulders. He was torn loose and thrown.

Stone is very hard, he discovered.

His head cracked against the temple's wall and suddenly he was flying in the cold, damp, cloud fields of the north under a never-setting sun.

Chapter 12

When the small shadow disappeared in the temple hallway, it took a moment for Aung to understand what he had seen. The damnable page wasn't in hiding. He was investigating!

He should have known—the page was nothing if not single-minded.

And potentially going to be discovered if Aung didn't get him out of here quickly.

The trouble was, the barest sound echoed in these stone corridors. Any whisper was amplified for everyone to hear as if the ancient builders did not believe in secrets. Even a sigh could become a north wind.

Glancing back at the storyteller—still deep in the trials of his heroes and heroines, but building toward climax—Aung slipped into the temple's darkness.

If he could edge down to where he'd seen Yamin, perhaps he could collect the page and get him back to the troupe. Then he could bring the others to stop this defiler of the temple—this thief. Surely Master Nu could help the thief understand the error of his ways.

He hugged the age-smoothed walls and tread carefully. A misplaced foot could crack stone and alert this sacrilegious man. A few steps down the ambulatory and he was where he thought he'd seen Yamin.

There was no sign of the page.

"I see you, man!" A strange voice boomed from the ceiling and seemed to come from all around.The noise filled the temple like thunder and echoed down the halls. "You will pay for defiling my temple!"

Aung jerked back against the wall. The man dropped his tools and leapt to his feet, guiltily looking for the source of the voice. Then his gaze fell and must have cut through Aung's shadows. His gaze widened.

Aung's jaw dropped in surprise. The defiler was Khin Moe, the dead boy's cousin—the one he had spoken to at the funeral.

Before Aung could say anything, the much younger man leapt. He slammed Aung back against the wall, his young hands throttling Aung's throat.

Strong hands. Deadly hands. Strong enough to break a boy's neck.

Aung clawed at them. He fought for breath. Khin Moe's hands were unrelenting.

His lungs cried for air, but there was none. He gouged at the youth's face, but Aung's fingers weren't strong. Khin Moe's hands held on and the temple was fading.

It was Aung's time to die. He sent an apology to Min Mahagiri. An aged singer had tried to uphold his end of the Great Nat's deal—to no avail.

Then through his shadowed vision something fell onto the young man's back. Khin Moe yelped, released Aung, and the singer collapsed.

Air. Blessed air. And then Khin Moe furiously threw something small at the stone temple wall.

C—rack came the sound of rending wood, planting despair in Aung's heart as the world went black.

§

Aung regained consciousness to the sound of a fight. He shoved himself up slowly and in the flicker of candlelight saw two overgrown shadows struggling against the cream-colored wall of the temple. One shadow was man sized. The other was the size of a giant. Fists from the smaller figure caught the giant in the middle. There were oomphs and unknown words that echoed like curses, but then the larger figure's fist found the smaller man's chin. The large figure caught the smaller and spun him around and slammed him against the wall. The smaller man suddenly went still and slumped to the floor just as a shout rose from the temple entrance. A flood of villagers streamed down the ambulatory, grabbed the giant Harold Heath, and shoved him against the wall.

As if he was the wrongdoer. Was he?

Suddenly Thura was beside Aung. "Master! Master, are you hurt? Let me help you!"

Aung shook his head, and pain shot through his skull so he regretted the movement. What had happened? Why had Harold Heath been fighting? Why was he in the temple?

From the back of the crowd, Master Nu shoved through the press of people to kneel beside the groaning man that Harold Heath had subdued.

The thief. Aung was certain that was right. He struggled to sit up again.

"This foreigner has attacked these men." Master Nu waved a hand in Aung's direction and then looked down the tunnel to where other villagers had been brought by the commotion. They were examining the candlelit damaged wall. Master Nu sprang to his feet. "Look what the foreigner has done! He tries to steal from the temple. He must be punished!"

A low growl arose from the crowd and it seemed to close ranks around Harold Heath.

"Stop!" Aung groaned and tried for his feet. His memories were hazy, but what Master Nu said wasn't the truth. He was certain of it.

Only with young Thura's strong arm around his waist did he make it to stand wavering on his own feet. He shook his head and would have fallen again, if not for Thura's steadying hand.

"That is not how it happened," Aung said, his voice slowly steadying. "This man," he pointed at Khin Moe, "attempted to steal the carving from the temple." He remembered Yamin's enlarged voice from the ceiling and wondered where the little page had got to. There had been that horrible, half-seen image of Yamin hitting the wall...and that terrible sound...

"When I tried to stop him, he attacked and strangled me—or tried to," Aung said. "If it had not been for Harold Heath, he would have killed me." And he was sure that Yamin had been involved somehow. The whole affair was muddled up in his head.

"He lies!" said the thief, still on the ground behind the shelter of Master Nu's robes.

"That cannot be the truth," Master Nu said. "I know this man. We all know him. He is the cousin of young Hlaing Htay. He would not hurt anyone."

Aung studied the young man on the dusty ambulatory floor and considered everything he knew. "There is more to this than an attempt to remove this carving tonight. There have been many carvings removed from other temples. Dhammayangyi has lost something from its doorways. I found missing carvings from other temples and there is an empty niche behind the puppet troupe's enclosure. I had thought this was done to please the king, but I have heard rumors of men willing to take these things and put them for sale—to the foreigners in Yangoon, or so I have heard."

He thought a moment. "Even our King Bodawpaya has commented on the voracious hunger of the foreigners who have overcome the Moghul princes. He fears all of Burma may be next." He lifted his chin at Harold Heath. "His kind are always hungry for things. His saddle bag carried Jataka stones and a small carving, but not from here, and tonight I know he was not involved. If he was, why would he have stopped this man from killing me just as Hlaing Htay was killed? I was half dead when the foreigner intervened."

Khin Moe glowered up at him. Master Nu spluttered.

"Neither of you had any love for young Hlaing Htay," Aung continued "You accused him of spying, and of threatening blackmail. What would you do if the very boys you had recruited to help you steal carvings suddenly turned on you?" He thought a moment. "Yes. That is how it was, I think—until young Hlaing Htay became remorseful. He had been raised by a grandfather who believed deeply in the spirits. Something that Khin Moe never did. Think about it, all of you. Young Hlaing Htay and his friend Lwin Kwye were expert climbers. What could be more perfect when trying to remove statues from difficult places? But if the lads then threatened to expose their partners, what do you think would happen? I cannot believe that someone like Khin Moe would stand by and allow that to happen."

There were murmurs in the crowd. Those holding Harold Heath appeared to ease their grip on the big man.

Aung studied the crowd and Master Nu. There were unfriendly glares cast in Aung's direction. Well, it must be done.

"His partners would not be happy, either," Aung said softly, but the ambulatory acoustics magnified his words.

"Partners?" Thura asked, as if on cue.

"Partners?" echoed the merchant whose pwe had been so poorly interrupted. "What partners? Surely this one worked alone?" He flicked his hand at Khin Moe, as if he could not bear to look at the young man.

Aung wobbled on his feet under all the unfriendly stares. He shook his head slowly. "Something like this would require more than one person. Certainly, it required those who would cut the statues loose. I suspect our friend, here, was responsible for removing a number of the carvings with the help of the boys, but for one man and two boys to cover all of Pagan—that seems difficult and there are others who have the need of money every bit as much as he did. For example, I know of a town that makes toddy wine." His gaze found and held the broad-shouldered man in the white shirt. "The sale of such things would bring welcome relief from the town's meagre income. It could even draw on the knowledge of the temples held by the community of nuns in the village."

"Nuns!" Master Nu sprang to his feet and stood close enough that Aung inhaled the scent of Nu's sour sweat. "Nuns would not see a temple defiled any more than I would!"

Aung rallied his strength and turned a baleful glare on the monk. The huge ambulatory felt like it swung around him and the sounds of the crowd were like over-loud breathing. It made his own breath hard to keep even and his head started pounding. His flesh was so cold he didn't think he would ever be warm again and the world itself was frozen under him. Where was Yamin? What had happened to him?

Then he caught the glint of Master Nu's black gaze and remembered where he was again. Aung drew himself up.

"But what if it was not seen as defilement?" He looked back to the crowd. "The king's own edict says that nats are no long to be propitiated—that their worship steers us away from the true Buddhist faith. There are those amongst the Sangha—the brethren of monks and the nuns—who agree. Like you, Master Nu. Like, I suspect, Daw Ma Kyi. How could it defile a temple to remove such things and sell them to the foreigners? Perhaps it even earns the monastery much needed funds—to mend damaged walls perhaps?"

"How dare you!" Master Nu caught Aung by the front of his shirt. "You wander into Pagan as if you are saviors! As if you are above everyone! As if you alone can solve this crime." He looked into the crowd. "Let me give you a different story. This one and his troupe of manikins are the source of all trouble and they bring trouble with them. They could have murdered that boy themselves and only claimed to have seen the nuns.

They could have been working with this one!" He pointed at Harold Heath. "It could have been this old man who tried to steal the carving from the temple and this one tried to stop him!" He motioned at Khin Moe.

Aung held his breath. It *was*, unfortunately, a plausible story.

"But the temple carvings were disappearing long before the puppet troupe arrived in Pagan." Htet Hla, the tea shop owner, stepped forward through the crowd. "And there are other witnesses to what has been happening." She produced a young boy from behind her. "Lwin Kwye, it is time. You must tell them what you know."

The town people and Master Nu gasped.

"Lwin Kwye!" Thura said. "The puppeteers have been looking everywhere for you!"

"As have these men's friends," Htet Hla said, motioning at Master Nu and Khin Moe. "If they had found him, there would have been a second body, but I have helped him stay hidden—until this evening when apparently the promise of a royal puppet troupe destroyed all sense of caution." She glowered affectionately down at him. "His grandmother was a great friend of mine. I have always seen my way to keep an eye on him."

"What do you know, boy?" asked the merchant.

Lwin Kwye looked up at all the adults waiting on what he had to say. He was a small lad with large, soft eyes and crafty hands that would surely do him well as a carver or artisan. If given the chance, the strength of his shoulders said he might even make a puppeteer. His thin throat worked and finally he nodded and pointed at Aung. "It's like he said. There was a man—a foreigner—and Khin Moe always sold to him, but it was the nuns and Master Nu who told us where to take from."

"You lie! I am your teacher!"

"But what have you been teaching, Master Nu?" Aung said.

The villagers closed in around Harold Heath again. Given what the boy said, it could be true. There *had* been that sense of recognition in the eyes of Master Nu when Aung had introduced Harold Heath and his father...

The father. Aung looked up and met Harold Heath's blue gaze. For all their strangeness, for all that had happened, and for all Aung's suspicions, there was no culpability there.

"The other foreigner. The man in black. He was here, earlier. Where is he now?"

Villagers ran to check and soon returned with the news that the Father Blackmoor was gone.

"He must be found! He had large saddle bags. Check them. Find where he has been staying," Aung cried.

Villagers flooded from the temple, leaving only the merchant and a few others, including Htet Hla and Lwin Kwye. They released Harold Heath and took Master Nu and Khin Moe into custody to take to the village headman's home along with the woman and boy as witnesses. It left Aung with Thura and Harold Heath. In the temple, the lone candle guttered and spat. Beyond the temple came the flare of lightning and the rumble of thunder and heavy rain falling.

Aung's legs sagged. He slumped against the wall and slid down to sitting.

"Master? Master, what do you need?"

Thura's words took a moment to register as Aung rested his head against the cold stone. He was so cold that he was shivering.

Then there came the scurrying of feet hurrying away and the giant's musty woolen scent filled his nose.

When he opened his eyes, Harold Heath was crouched beside him. "Thank you for standing to my defense."

"And I thank you for saving my life," Aung managed, though English words were hard to dig out of his brain. His head throbbed so that it felt like the dragon drum beat inside his skull.

"Your apprentice is bringing help," Harold Heath said.

Aung barely nodded. It would feel so good to simply fall asleep and never wake to the pain of his neck and the back of his head.

Now he knew how a chicken felt. And that was a thought he knew Yamin would enjoy.

"Aung?"

The voice seemed to come from so far away.

"Aung!" more insistent.

He managed to open his eyes. "I found this. I believe he is a friend of yours, though what he is doing here is beyond me."

Shadows played across the big man's face and seemed to catch in the blue of his eyes. Aung gradually focused on what Harold Heath held. Small, with blue pantaloons and a sequined vest. Two ponytails bobbing over a painted face.

Yamin. Harold Heath had once more returned the page to him. He held out his arms and accepted the comforting weight of his small charge, then his eyes fluttered closed again.

Chapter 13

Aung woke, breath caught in his throat, from a deep, painful sleep where he had spent years searching for something—something never found. It was small and precious and lost to him and he had to get it back or the world would never be the same again.

Overhead was a dimly lit palm thatch roof. A bamboo wall stood beside him and a bamboo mat lay underneath. The bamboo mat was normal, but the wall and roof were not. At most there should be a cloth curtain; most often there was nothing at all. Blue sky in the day and the stars at night. That was where home should be.

Where was he?

A rumble of thunder and the rustle of rain on the palm-thatched roof said he was better off where he was.

He tried to sit up and groaned at the pounding throb in his head. The movement had loosed a woodpecker in his skull, and his neck felt too weak to hold up his head at all. He ground his fists into his eyes and steadied his breath. Breathe in. Breathe out. This, too, would pass, just as all things passed away in this life.

Like the boy, Hlaing Htay.

Like the nat figures that had decorated the walls.

Like Yamin?

His heart beat too hard in his chest and he remembered too well what he'd searched for in his dreams—a small grinning imp of a page. Had he been destroyed by that fiend? How could a child kill a child? A brother kill a brother? The idea filled him with revulsion. Is that what his people were becoming? To kill simply to protect an illicit scheme. And not once, either, if Htet Hla's tale of her husband's death meant anything. Khin Moe and his compatriots had been working at Dhammayangyi for some time.

He had to know about Yamin. His tiny form had felt so empty when Harold Heath had returned it to Aung. No more than a bundle of wood chips and string. Had Yamin's spirit gone, as the Min's had? It might mean the end of the troupe, but his fear was more for his small friend. Surprisingly, he liked the little page.

His observations of the world were *interesting*—not the jaded views of an old man.

And he was astute, as well. Yamin had been closer than they'd thought when he'd proposed that a child could kill a child, for Khin Moe was only a few years older—perhaps Thura's age—or less.

He rolled over on the bamboo mat and found he was on a sleeping platform at the rear of a stilted house. It took more effort than it should to push himself up to sitting and place his hoary old feet on the floor. Then he stood and shuffled to the door that looked out onto a night-darkened courtyard. To the east the sky showed the first hope of morning.Rain-slicked bougainvillea swayed in the darkness along the courtyard walls. A htaung tree thrashed its branches in a storm wind. Voices and firelight came from the dry space below the floorboards. Most of the voices he recognized. Saya Lin, as ever, making plans for moving on. U Myint speaking quietly to the dragon drummer. Thura telling a story— that boy could have been a storyteller if Aung hadn't stolen him away to become a singer. The others—his chosen family. And a woman.

Htet Hla.

Wobbling, he stepped into the rain and started down the ladder and then suddenly there were steadying hands there to aid him. Thura helped him into the comfortable shelter under the house and to a seat close to the fire.

Saya Lin crossed the fire to settle beside him. "You gave us a scare, old friend. You were so cold and so still, I feared we might lose you." There was real concern in the wizened puppet master's gaze, so perhaps things were not so far gone between them. That was the thing about people—there was evil, but also great good in all of them.

Aung nodded. "I think I scared myself. I had not expected young Khin Moe to come at me like that. My head is still rattled and my neck—" Gingerly he touched it and was surprised at the jolt of pain.

"It's black and blue, Master," Thura said. "Almost as black as Khin Moe's heart and those of the others."

"A very pretty hue in places," Saya Lin said with a smile.

"And what of the culprits? Have they all been apprehended?"

Saya Lin shrugged as if it did not concern him. "Khin Moe and the monk you know. The big man from the southern village was caught—apparently his work was an attempt to undermine the headman—an unpleasant man who owns the village toddy palm.

Apparently, the big man kept Daw Ma Kyi and her nuns almost hostages in their home unless they identified suitable carvings for him. When the nuns found the body they dared not help for fear of reprisals on the older nuns at the village. As for the foreigner, he was last seen heading toward Amarapura. I'm sure the king and he will get along famously." The old puppeteer smiled grimly.

Aung took it all in. A case solved again, however shakily, and just like the others there was little satisfaction in knowing who had done the killing. He chose to think of other things. "I take it we have Htet Hla to thank for our fine circumstances?" Aung asked and nodded at the tea shop owner. "I thank you. It would have been far less pleasant to convalesce in the downpour."

"We could not have our star investigator left in the rain. It was an easy choice to offer my home as it is not so far from the pwe location."

He gave thanks to her and looked back to Saya Lin. "The puppets were brought here?"

Saya Lin nodded. "All our things. There are too many thieves and brigands in these parts, it seems. Those who would desecrate temples would think nothing of stealing our small friends. I shall be happy to leave here tomorrow morning."

"Harold Heath returned one to me this evening," Aung said, thinking of Yamin.

"He is safe and well," Saya Lin murmured. "The trunks are stored in a bier just inside the wall."

A great weight lifted from his shoulders and he inhaled deeply, fighting the tears that welled in his eyes.

"Thura? Would you show me?"

His apprentice glanced from Aung to Saya Lin. The puppet master and leader of the troupe shook his head, but Thura stood anyway and helped Aung up again. Together they stepped out of the shelter into the pouring rain. The air was fresh, the deluge cool, and Aung held his face to the sky for a moment, though his poor injured neck complained at the movement. This was the nats' way of smiling, he was sure. He had found and stopped the destruction of their images in the temple.

"Just let Yamin be whole," he whispered.

A small bier had been built inside the wall to store food and equipment for Htet Hla's small tea shop. Most of this had been pushed into a corner to allow space for the troupe's equipment. The lone exception was the huge dragon drum hung on a large carved naga dragon that stood in the rain, draped in thick cloths for protection.

The rain stopped when they stepped under the thatched roof, but a steady cascade of drops sluiced off the small structure's front and sides. The puppet trunks were stacked four high. Thura went to one stack and started removing trunks.

"Saya Lin did not want to take any chances that Yamin would leave again," he explained as he finally uncovered the last of the trunks—Yamin's. "He fears that you have created a monster."

Aung shook his head and a bolt of pain made him wish that he hadn't. "Monsters are never created. We all carry our monsters within us. It is a question of whether we lose our humanity and let the monster out."

"But Yamin isn't human," Thura said as he flipped the basket lid open.

"Isn't he? Haven't you noticed the change in him? He was... disturbed by this case and most disturbed by the evil of the children toward each other. I think he may have begun to think of himself as a boy. Certainly, he saw some affinity. Perhaps he worried that he could do such things and so finding the killer became more important than anything."

The small page's wooden body lay in his basket, his arms at his sides, his clothing hurriedly tidied but still carrying the dust and grime of the temple. His long black ponytails were loose and one sequined holder was almost torn in two.

There was no puff of incense. No stretch of arms, and no charming, impish grin.

"Are you sure there was no damage?" Aung asked, a horrible sinking feeling filling his chest.

"Zeya and U Myint both checked him over. They say there is nothing broken."

Except his heart—if yoke thei had such things.

"Would you keep watch and make sure no one disturbs us?" Aung asked.

Thura nodded and stepped out into the darkness and the rain. He was a good boy, that one. The kind Yamin should emulate. Aung bent low over the wicker basket and inhaled the sandalwood scent of the puppet's heritage.

"Yamin?" he asked softly.

The little page didn't stir, as if he was long lost beyond the singer and the worst of Aung's dreams had come true.

"Yamin, please come back. I, for one, have need of you and your bravery and your quick mind. You knew before I did what that man had done. You are very wise for one who appears so young."

The rain rattled in the palm fronds and plopped in the puddles that had formed on the ground. The wind sighed in the trees and Aung was sure he heard the voices of the *taw sauns*—the nat-guardians of trees. Trees such as Yamin had once been part of.

He reached into the basket and caught the page's small hand. "Yamin, truly, I miss you. Things would never be the same if you were lost—haven't I told you that again and again?"

"And haven't I told you your breath smells of betel and old rice!" Yamin's eyes flashed open at the same time as the fragrance of incense filled the bier. The little page leapt to his feet to face Aung with his hands on his hips.

Then his lips began to quiver. "I—I thought he'd killed you," he said so softly Aung almost couldn't hear. "I saw him hurting you and I didn't know what to do, and it was all my fault because I tried to deal with him alone and didn't wait for you and what I did actually made things worse because he attacked you."

He plopped down, cross-legged in the center of his basket, shaking his head. "It's true what everyone has said. I only cause problems and I nearly got you killed. I'm every bit as bad as those human boys." He looked bleakly up at Aung. "I thought maybe it would be better to remain in the cloud fields of the north and not cause anymore harm."

"And leave me bored to tears? And without an investigative partner?" Aung shook his head and shot the page a glance. "It would be very hard for me to bear."

"It would? After all the injury I caused you?"

"You saved me, Yamin. You've saved me in more ways than you know. The world around us changes and the people lose their way, but that will never happen to me because I have you."

"So the case was solved, then?" As usual, the little page managed to change the direction of his thoughts like a butterfly.

"Yes, I suppose it was, though whether the humans will act on it is another matter. The culprits were a group of people."

"The monk Master Nu, the big tree-climber from the nun's village, the dead boy's cousin. And the giant, of course." Yamin enumerated them on his small fingers.

Aung shook his head. "You are partially right and partially wrong. The monk, the tree-climber, and the cousin were all involved as were the dead boy and his friend Lwin Kwye." He held up his hand to stop Yamin's astonished cry. "Yes, the two boys were accomplices in stealing the statues from the temples, but they decided to blackmail the adults and so young Hlaing Htay was dealt with. Lwin Kwye fled, but returned last night under the urging of his grandmother's friend. He is telling quite a story to those who will listen."

"And the giant?" Yamin asked.

"Innocent, or at least as innocent as any of these foreigners are. It was his Father Blackmoor who was inciting the ravages in the temples. I am not even sure whether Harold Heath knew what was happening. You know, it was Harold Heath who returned you to me in the pahto. You had been lost after Khin Moe threw you off. Harold Heath could have easily taken you—again. It was also Harold Heath who described seeing the man from the toddy palms in an oxen cart. Remember?"

Yamin nodded. Then he adamantly shook his head. "I still do not trust him."

"And you are probably right not to. But for now, I am happy that things are good between us, and that you are safely stowed in your basket."

Frowning, Yamin patted the straw and cotton that made up his bedding. Then he looked up brightly. "I think I am coming to appreciate that it is a good basket. And now I think I will return to the cloud fields, for my head still aches where I hit the wall." His gaze narrowed a little as he studied Aung. "You would be well advised to get some rest yourself. You have circles under your eyes and your neck is a most unbecoming shade of purple."

"I will do what you say," Aung said, standing. He motioned to Thura to replace the baskets into position once Yamin had laid his head down and the scent of incense had once more sweetened the air.

Beyond the bier the rain was slacking, and eastward the sky had lightened, placing an apricot crescent into the heavens. Birds filled the moist air with their songs and the rain drip-drip-dripped from the violet-colored bougainvillea blooms.

Saya Lin met him at the base of the ladder to the house. Beyond him, the troupe was rousing from around the fire and gathering their things. "Come, old friend. It is time to go. The boatman waits and so does Yangoon. The merchant has granted us our fee in exchange for the capture of the killer."

Later, aboard the small, shallow-drafted craft with blue plaid sails set and long oars stowed, the troupe set sail southward. Aung was seated next to the puppet baskets in the center of the boat in the shadow cast by the great dragon drum. The boatman allowed the strong currents of the Ayeyarwady to carry them away from Pagan town, but as they passed the massive temples that crowded the river with their huge corncob spires, there came a spot where the road ran directly along the river.

There, a gray horse trotted under a pale-haired rider who seemed to know who passed him by. He lifted his arm in a wave that was somewhere between farewell and a greeting as he kicked his horse faster. Cantering, they headed south.

Toward the Andaman Sea. Toward Yangoon and its harbors.

Join K.L. Abrahamson/Karen L. Abrahamson's Mystery Readers!

If you'd like more of K.L. Abrahamson's mysteries, join other mystery enthusiasts and receive a free novel, a novella, and an award-nominated short story.

AND/OR

Join K.L. Abrahamson/Karen L. Abrahamson's Fantasy Readers!

If you'd like more of K.L. Abrahamson's fantasies, join other fantasy enthusiasts and receive three free novels.

Go to www.karenlabrahamson.com and

click on your preference to get your free books!

Don't go yet. Please leave a review!

If you enjoyed this book (and even if you didn't), it would be immensely helpful if you would leave a review at your favorite on-line retailer or on Goodreads (or both). Reviews help gain me visibility and they can bring my books to the attention of other readers who may enjoy them.

Thank you so much!

The Aung and Yamin Mysteries

What do a mischievous, spirit-imbued puppet and a wizened puppet singer have in common? In this case, it's solving mysteries.

In 19th Century Burma, foreigners are slowly sinking their teeth into the Burmese kingdom while living spirits still walk the land. Where they meet, ancient belief systems clash. So, too, do those who adhere to tradition and those who have forgotten powers far older than Buddha. In this mysterious land, wandering puppet troupes and their magic marionettes are the only source of news and social commentary. It makes the troupes important. It makes them dangerous to the king. It makes their lives risky enough without assuming the task of investigating murder and mayhem along their way.

Welcome to the perilous world of Aung Aung the puppet singer and his accomplice, the not so faithful, and occasionally not so helpful, puppet, Yamin.

Books in the Series:
Death By Effigy (Guardbridge Books)
A Death In Passing
Death In Umber

I hope their adventures bring you wonder and a smile.

About the Author

Karen L. Abrahamson is a well-traveled writer who has explored cultures and countries around the world but British Columbia, Canada is her favorite place to come back to. She is the author of literary, mystery, romantic and fantasy fiction including the highly regarded Cartographer fantasy series. She lives on the west coast of Canada with two Bengal cats that aren't quite as well traveled as she is.

When she isn't writing she can be found with a camera and backpack in fabulous locations around the world.

To find out more about her and her writing, visit www.karenlabrahamson.com

Fantasy and Mystery by
Karen L. Abrahamson

Mystery (Writing as K.L. Abrahamson)
Through Dark Water

Fantasy Mystery
Aung and Yamin Series
Death By Effigy (Guardbridge Books)
A Death in Passing
Death in Umber

*The Cartographer Universe
(in chronological order)*
The Warden of Power
Impossible
The Cartographer's Daughter
The American Geological Survey Series:
Afterburn
Aftershock
Aftermath
Afterimage
Terra Incognita
Terra Infirma
Terra Nueva

Other Fantasy Novels
Ice Dragon
Emberstone
Mutable Things
The Crystal Courtesan

Here's a Sneak Peak at a new Alternate History mystery,

After Yekaterina coming Spring 2018

Chapter 1

My parents named me Yekaterina after Our Lady. Yekaterina is my secret name, the one I wear on my heart. To everyone else I am Kadija, after the Prophet's first wife, in case the invaders find us again.

My village has no name. It sits at the base of the Tian Shan mountains like a tick on the neck of a mangy dog. It has always existed, according to the elders, though its population has waxed and waned.

In the night, in the snug warmth of the hide yurt my father's father built outside the village's mud walls, my parents whisper tales of a different day. The days when Our Lady Yekaterina reigned like a goddess in her golden palace, until the heathen Saracen raged through our country. Of how, out of the ashes of Muscovy she rose again and escaped to lead us through pestilence and famine on a march so horrible most of us died in the winters. It was her strength that flowed into our veins, her will that kept us alive and she loved us as if we were her children—until her strength ran out.

It was at her death, when all hope died and the warring captains fought for her simple robe and scepter, that my grandparents fled, for the pestilence had returned and our numbers dwindled further. My grandparents and their friends came here, to the country of Fergana, the promised land.

The tattered history textbook page caught in the wind as Detektiv Alexander Kazakov stood at the edge of the crime scene. The walls of mountains to the south and east were white today, pouring cold air into the wide Fergana Valley, and he pulled the karakul fur collar of his coat tighter around his neck. At four o'clock the October light was faded. Winter was coming. The aspen and walnut trees had dropped their gilded leaves almost overnight and the golden geese formed 'V' phalanxes overhead as if heavy bombers ranged south.

Again.

Except the geese were nigh-on silent, just the distant haunting honking as they dared the mountain passes that kept the Chinese if not at bay, at least at a distance. The war between the Ottomans to the west and the Chinese to the east had been going on so long, it was almost impossible to imagine a time without war, though the feints and attacks overhead had waned these past few years. History said that the Germans had eaten into the remains of what had once been Holy Russia until they met their allies, the Ottomans. The Anglos and Germans had joined together to overcome the small French general. But Russia was no more—as the old text book bore testament to. And the tiny democracy that was Fergana had grown out of Russia's remains and prepared to hold back invaders, but the invaders didn't come.

Not yet, not yet, blew the wind.

The original Yekaterina's aspirations led to her downfall.

"And what did you aspire to that lost you your life, little one?" he said, studying the photo identification in his hand. The only answer was the rush of traffic from Suvarov Way just beyond the line of trees that blocked the broad boulevards of new Fergana.

He ducked under the police tape and trod the desiccated grass of Potemkin Park, named after the man who had been the original Yekaterina's strength until the Ottomans slew him. The park lay along the river on the eastern edge of the city center amongst three-story walk-ups that were slowly being eaten up as New Moscow's business core grew. In warmer weather the place would be filled with young couples and with mothers besieged by flocks of children. Now it was almost empty, which accounted for the body only being spotted late this afternoon by an officer on patrol.

The girl lay naked, face up under the cold October sun with the white-clad M.E. crouched beside her. The blue sky tinged the pallor of her skin. Her eyes were milky white as if she'd been here for some time. A skein of pale hair fanned around her head and twisted around her neck. Her pale pink mouth was half open to the air as if she would drink it in. A northern girl, in police parlance, a true Russian. Not the dark-haired beauties of the area's original Kyrgyz and Uzbek tribes.

He glanced down at her ID locked in a plastic bag. Kazakov had found it in a bundle of carefully folded clothing—slim, gray skirt and a pink fluffy sweater— just inside the police tape along with the history book and a school diary schedule. No one had touched it except for him. Yekaterina Weber. German sounding name. Strange, or perhaps not given the Anglo-German Empire's arrogant citizens apparently had a God-given right to travel wherever they wanted these days. She was sixteen years old.

"What have we got?" He knelt beside the M.E., Dr. Khalil Khan.

A small brown man with a thick thatch of dark hair and black, slightly slitted eyes, Khan was a Muslim anomaly—a direct descendant of Fergana's historic people in the usually orthodox Christian government machine. He glanced up at Kazakov, then down at the I.D. The victim was lucky to have the little dark man attending. Where most government M.E.s didn't give a damn about their jobs, Khalil Khan was skilled—and he cared.

"That her?" Dr. Khan asked.

"Yekaterina Weber, yes," Kazakov said.

Khan rolled the body over on its side so Kazakov could see the deep lash marks and a puncture wound on her back. He let her slump back down on the grass and her face turned to Kazakov as if to ask him a question.

How long are you going to leave me here? How long before Our Lady Yekaterina rises again? How long before the legends come true?

This was Russia, or what remained of it. Even two hundred plus years since Yekaterina made the mistake of trying to take the Black Sea's Crimean peninsula from the Ottomans, couldn't erase all that history and yearnings of a people. But then this was a people descended mostly from soldiers, servants and serfs. Not intelligentsia. Tales of the old hag Baba Yaga, the foolish priest and glass slippers were still told and perhaps even believed. He'd been raised on such magical fictions. In them Baba Yaga was both the witch who ate children and their savior. A lot like the true Yekaterina. With such creatures, how and whom did one trust?

Dearest Yekaterina, he thought as he studied the girl: It could take a long time, if it happens at all.

"The lashes look like they were perimortem. Whip most likely. Done with anger? The puncture wound probably killed her. It was most likely a knife-like instrument. She may not have died here."

Kazakov nodded. "Not enough blood on the ground. Even though the ground's not frozen, there should be some sign of a pool. So, the killing was emotionally motivated. When the whipping wasn't enough our murderer killed her."

Dr. Khan nodded. "You're learning." He lifted her arm. "By the lack of rigor I'd say that she'd been here a few hours at most, but it's harder to judge with the cold. It could be as long as twelve hours. You can see the process has started in the tightness of the eyelids and the jut of the jaw." He nodded down at the girl. "Funny how a smile makes all the difference." The girl in the government school ID was dressed in a pink fluffy sweater and her hair was swept back behind her ears. A broad white smile was aimed at the camera.

Khan was right. The smile made her look like a school girl, ready for her future.

But in the grass, she was just another Yekaterina: past czarina, long dead diarist, they were all just dead on this chill October morning.

§

In the cold concrete office of the New Moscow *politseyshiyuchastok*, the police station, Kazakov sat with the girl's school book and identification open before him. The drafty room housed ten detectives, the small city's entire squad, dealing with all forms of crime from drugs to murder in the city center and old city. Other squads, housed elsewhere, dealt with crime in the suburbs and still another specialty unit dealt with corporate crime. Seven of the room's nine other cold metal desks were unoccupied at the moment. Apparently, most cases had been solved by six o'clock today.

The two other desks were occupied by Antonov and Alenin, the A and A team—partners who had worked together the past ten years. Antonov was a granite block of a man with sullen blue eyes and scowling, downturned lips that could turn themselves upright at the blackest of humor. But a frown and a black sense of humor weren't something to be held against him— Kazakov shared them—as did most detectives in New

Moscow. Antonov was a fine investigator who had graduated from training a year before Kazakov—and never failed to remind Kazakov of it.

His partner, Alenin, was five years Kazakov's junior and the antithesis of Antonov's body type—tall, with an athelete's broad shoulders and lean muscle slowly gathering the weight of middle age. He had pale blue eyes and a ready smile that offset the dourness of his partner.

Kazakov sighed and inhaled the stink of cold tea and the cheap unfiltered Ottoman cigarettes preferred by the squad and most of the country. He had quit smoking himself, or so he told himself, though he still kept a single cigarette in his wallet against emergencies.

"That was a deep sigh, friend," Alenin said looking up from where he was reading a document over Antonov's shoulder. "Have you finally found a girl who will have you?" He grinned.

It was the same teasing refrain that had hounded Kazakov since he and his wife split up and he hadn't immediately taken another woman.

"I suppose you could say that," Kazakov played along. "Except this one is sixteen years old and dead of stab wounds." He met Alenin's gaze. "Who else will have her?"

"Maudlin bastard," Antonov muttered. "Let him have her, Sergei. We have other fish to fry." The big man gave a small nod to Kazakov. They had worked a few cases together long ago. There was still respect between them, though their outlook on many things had diverged.

Kazakov turned back to his evidence. He sipped his cold, sweet tea as he considered. The school book was one he remembered from his own childhood, a treasured diary of one of the first generations of Russian refugees to make the lush fields of the Fergana Valley their home.

The flood of migrants had come at a price. The traditional Kyrgyz and Uzbek villagers and their animistic beliefs had at first been welcoming, but then had been pushed out by the sheer numbers of displaced people who had come east. Those villagers had taken to the higher mountains, while a Muslim minority had stayed as the desperate Russians settled around them.

The Russians had been starving and dying from the plague that descended on them after the Ottoman war destroyed all infrastructure and food sources. It was on that desperate diaspora following the Tea Road across the continent that blessed Yekaterina gave the decimated remains of her people the gift of democracy for their petty states. For a few of them, like those in

Fergana, the gift had held. Yekaterina had always held that Russians were different from all others.

But why was the girl carrying this particular book? It was a two-hundred-year-old book, read to elementary school children and Yekaterina Weber was certainly older than twelve.

And what was she doing in Potemkin Park? Less than twelve hours dead at most, Khan had said. That would mean that she'd been out before five in the morning. An unusual time for a girl that age. Most teenagers preferred to be up in late morning. And why left there and naked? It was as if the killer was making some point. He would have to wait on Khan's report to know if it was a sex crime, but the lack of clothing suggested it.

First things first. He needed to contact the family, not a job he enjoyed when the news wasn't good. Shoving himself up from his desk he lumbered over to the small desk in the corner, and slumped into the seat. The massive machine was the latest investigative tool provided to their office, courtesy of the city council.

It was a huge, gray, steel-covered block imported from the Germans, almost as tall as a man, with ugly metal on three sides and what looked like a twenty-inch television screen on the front with a keyboard in a small depression beneath the screen.

Bending to look at the keyboard, he typed in Yekaterina Weber, hit the red *send* button and leaned back in the chair. It groaned under his bulk for though he had always kept fit through his outdoor activities, he had grown lazy in his exercise these past five years since his fortieth birthday. Not for the first time today, he had the urge to smoke.

Ping.

The machine had things to tell him like a fairy tale fish or birds that held the secret truth. He hit the blue receive button. A list of names appeared with the top name in bold, the most likely match for the requested name. The length of the list surprised him. It seemed there were more German Webers residing in Fergana than he'd realized. For a moment, like a shiver at a memory, the realization made him uncomfortable.

Some said the feeling came when someone walked over your grave.

§

The home address listed on the government database had been pulled from government school records and existed beyond the large eight-story towers of the business heart of Fergana and beyond the brightly-painted domed concrete replica of Saint Basil's Cathedral in the middle of New Moscow. Beyond the walk-up apartments encircling Potemkin

Park, a new area had been planted with young trees at the curb. When the trees were grown this area would be a paradise compared to the flat, grassland steppes of the countryside.

Neat rows of steep-roofed houses with faux-wood concrete sides were physical echoes of the dacha homes the Russian people had left behind long ago—or at least what they believed them to be. Neat, pocket-sized yards held small vegetable gardens that were now faded and tattered brown with the fall. Here and there a last wizened tomato blushed forgotten and withered in the cool.

The Weber yard was surrounded by a hip-high concrete block fence like a half-hearted fortress in the midst of the neighborhood. The yard itself was mostly fallow though a few turnips and winter kale grew at the ends of regimented raised beds that looked newly turned. A small stool sat next to the door with a trowel and a set of gardening gloves, the gloves neatly pulled inside of each other. Everything in its place.

The porch was swept, the door newly painted, so slick and shiny red he wondered it didn't come off on his knuckles at his knock. The sounds of footfall echoed within and then the curtain stirred on the window beside the door. There was a moment of hesitation and then the door opened. A woman stood there, slim, with Yekaterina's silken blond hair darkened slightly by the years. It was twisted back from her face into a precise figure eight. She was tall for a woman, almost five-foot-nine in her low boxy heels with the buckles over the instep. She wore a slim-fitting tweed skirt and a brown cardigan—buttoned—over a crisp white blouse buttoned up to her throat.

"Yes?" Her eyes were guarded and she held the door as if she planned to slam it shut at the first sign of danger. As if she did not trust strangers.

"Detektiv Kazakov of the Fergana Politseyshiy." He showed her his identification. "You are Mrs. Weber?"

"Not Weber anymore. It is Bure. My first husband passed away and I remarried." She nodded, but her hand came up to her collar. "Is something wrong? My husband..."

Bure. The name meant something...

"May I come in?" There was something wrong with her response. The cold air of the afternoon swirled around his shoulders. She must feel it, but she seemed frozen where she stood. And no mention of her daughter. Odd.

Finally, she nodded and stepped aside. He ducked his head to enter and found himself inside— history. Wooden floors and walls gleamed as if someone regularly waxed them. The familiar scents of beetroot, tea and a slight hint of something sweet and spicy. To one side of the door a small parlor was dominated by a heavy ornate couch with embroidered cushions and a high, wingback chair covered in crimson damask. A fireplace mantle was filled with old family photos in silver frames that showed Mrs. Bure and a tall pale man who looked vaguely familiar. Others showed a younger Yekaterina in a frothy white dress that was typical of religious ceremonies, and a much younger version of the blonde man with an older version of himself, and an elegant blonde-haired woman who looked strangely similar to Mrs. Bure. His father and mother, maybe.

An antique crucifix hung in a corner, and in a niche in the wall hung what looked like a gold-gilt icon of the Virgin. It looked old. It looked genuine. It looked like something you would see in the treasury section of the Fergana Museum. For all the middle class outer trappings of their house, this family clearly had come from old wealth. And had brought it with them. Not a soldier, servant or serf.

He turned to Mrs. Bure and nodded at the icon. "A lovely piece. It is old, correct?"

She gave a single nod. "It was in my husband's family—all they brought out of old Russia."

He didn't quite believe her, but nodded. "Perhaps you should have a seat. This visit, it is about your daughter."

"Yekaterina?" She perched on the edge of the overwhelming couch and, if anything, her pale skin went almost the color of her dead daughter's flesh. "You've found her, then."

"Found her?"

"My husband reported her missing two days ago."

And that was impossible because when he entered the girl in the computer a flag for a missing person's case would have shown against her name.

"Do you know who he spoke to?" Kazakov asked. It was not unheard of that an officer was slow in entering information in the police information system...

She shook her head and the couch seemed to consume her. "What is this about? What has happened? Is Yekaterina all right?"

Finally, she asked the right question. Stranger and stranger. Why did her concern leap so quickly to her husband when she had a missing daughter? He took a deep breath and took the liberty of sitting down in the chair. "Mrs. Bure, when was the last time you saw your daughter?"

Her gaze fell to her hands. "It was Friday at supper. We were at the table and my husband scolded her. She was acting silly—almost giddy. My husband told her to mind her table manners or she could go to her room." Mrs. Bure bit her lip almost as if she knew what was coming. "She chose her room," she whispered.

These were the times he hated his job. The disaster. The pain that would overwhelm a loved one's eyes. But there was no use in delaying. It had to be done. "Mrs. Bure. I regret to inform you, but we found your daughter's body this morning in Potemkin Park. She had been stabbed. Yekaterina is dead."

"No." She shook her head. "That cannot be."

He reached across a small coffee table and caught her hand. "I am sorry, but it was her. She had her identification."

She went statue still, her face rigid. Then she yanked her hand away and stood. "No. No. Not Yekaterina. No." She paced the floor between the mantel and the door then stopped abruptly, still dry-eyed. "I must call my husband."

Kazakov stood. "A good idea. While you do, may I examine your daughter's room?"

She met his gaze, her lip quivering almost as if she was angry. "At the top of the stairs. The second door on the right." Then she left him for the back of the house that must be the kitchen.

Kazakov clumped up the stairs, considering. Most mothers would be in tears. Most mothers would be with him right now, sobbing about how their daughter was a good girl, demanding to know how and where and why this had happened and who would do something like this to their child. At the top of the stairs he paused to listen. Silence ticked around him in the darkened hallway, but from downstairs came the sound of harsh whispers. They rose and fell in the staccato of anger. Not grief, but fury.

§

The second room on the right had a closed door, but daylight placed long panels of light on the hall floor through the others. The first room on his left was clearly the parents'. Kazakov ducked his head inside. A double bed with quilted cover in a patchwork of shades of red. A curtained window. Built-in drawers along one wall. A wood heater against the winter cold and another orthodox icon hung on the wall. This one did not have the gold gilt of the one downstairs, but the lustrous paint said it was still old. Neat. Tidy. Well cared for.

He went down the hall to Yekaterina's room and opened the door.

The spice he'd detected at the front door caught him full in the face and he shook himself at the heady scent. It was like catching a face full of church brazier incense. Was the girl very religious? The body hadn't worn a crucifix, but there had been that photo in the white dress.

He stepped inside. A girl's room. Magazine pages of the latest shaggy-headed boy-band from Anglia taped to the wall. A narrow bed with a blue bedspread under the window. A desk. A straight-backed spindle chair. A small bookcase filled with books.

Closing the door behind him, he stood there hoping to get a feel for his victim, but from the look of things Yekaterina Weber was a typical schoolgirl. He opened the drawers of her desk but found only paper and pens—odd in itself. Didn't girls usually stuff odd sundry things into such places? There was nothing that told of Yekaterina or her friendships here.

The closet gave no more clues: a few straight cut skirts like her mother wore. Blouses. A sweater of navy blue. No pink fluffy sweater. Nothing like that at all. As if the pink sweater next to her body was special? Perhaps something she purchased herself because it made her feel pretty, while these clothes bore the straight-laced, utilitarian stamp of being purchased by her mother?

The bookcase held novels and school books. There was a slim empty space that he would bet his paycheck had once held the slim diary of Yekaterina of the yurts. He checked each of the remaining books, but found nothing. Where were her school notebooks? The binders teenagers used? She was in school. There had to be something of that kind.

He checked under the bed, but there was nothing there, not even dust. When he stepped out of the room, her mother was waiting.

"My husband will be home in a few minutes. He would like you to wait for him."

He nodded. "She has a very neat room. Unusual in a teenager."

Her chin lifted a little. "I expect my child to have high standards."

"I see." He nodded. "Does she keep a briefcase or a school backpack? I noticed that there are no school notebooks in the room."

Mrs. Bure went still. "She had one. It was a blue courier bag—the latest fashion. We got it for her last Christmas."

"And it is not in the house?" he asked.

"If it is not in her room, then it is not here." Her closed expression did not leave room for more questions.

His footsteps sounded hollow as he went down the stairs after her and soon a black Ziln limousine pulled up at the curb. Kazakov stiffened by the parlor window as a man climbed out of the front and held the door for a passenger. Bure. Kazakov remembered, now. Bure was a government functionary who was now being groomed for something greater. The newly formed Reformation Party had great things planned for him. Great enough to command a car and driver to bring him home.

Boris Bure was a man of middle height who seemed to command the hallway as soon as he entered. Perhaps it was his breadth of shoulder. Perhaps it was the rigid way he held his ramrod-straight back and white-haired head. Perhaps it was the metallic scent that came with him when he entered the room, as if he generated an electric charge. He had pale blue eyes and large white teeth that he exposed almost as a warning as he shook Kazakov's hand. Even though Bure was a good six inches shorter than Kazakov's six-foot-two, Bure seemed to look him eye-to-eye.

"What's this all about then? I reported Yekaterina missing two days ago and haven't spoken to a detective since and now you arrive telling my wife her daughter is dead."

Her daughter. Not his.

Kazakov bowed his head. "I am sorry to bring this bad news. Yekaterina's body was found in Potemkin Park this afternoon. She was murdered."

Her mother's hand came to her mouth as if she finally believed. Bure did nothing as if letting the news settle in. Then he nodded.

"Terrible news. Terrible." He caught his wife in a hug. "I know how this must upset you, love." He patted her back as if she might break, but if Kazakov was waiting for emotion in Bure's voice, it wasn't there.

The man made no move to take them back into the parlor either. It was more as if he expected Kazakov to leave.

"Mr. Bure, your wife tells me that you last had dinner with Yekaterina on Friday. Can you tell me about that?"

Bure shrugged, still holding his wife. "We ate. She was being foolish. I told her she could either act like a proper lady or she could go to her room."

Kazakov nodded and made a note of Bure's statement. "Can you tell me what she was doing that was so foolish?"

Bure and his wife looked at each other.

"It was nothing. She was talking nonsense."

"What, precisely, did she say?"

Bure released his wife to turn to Kazakov. "Detektiv, do I look like a man who would remember foolishness? Now my wife has had an awful shock. I would like to tend to her. Perhaps you could leave us in peace in this time of grief."

Bure eased past Kazakov and opened the door, inviting him to leave. Kazakov had gotten as much as he was going to from this odd couple, but it was stranger still that they did not want more from him. Now he just had to determine what this oddity meant.

§

It was two-thirty the next afternoon on his way to an appointment at Yekaterina's school that his radio crackled and he was called to the second body.

This one was on the far side of New Moscow, in the old Islamic quarter. Square mud and stucco houses leaned together around hidden central courtyards. Once the houses had been the graceful villas of the Muslim caravan merchants, for the Silk and Tea Roads had both wound through Fergana generations ago, but now each house held four or five impoverished families; it seemed the new Russian economy had no place for Muslim employees. Television antennas and clotheslines filled the flat roof tops. Narrow streets barely wide enough for a single car wound through the maze of buildings, the streets still sometimes blocked by a donkey carrying burlap bags of limes or an enterprising businessman who had spread his goods under awnings into the street.

Children scattered through the streets at the sight of his sedan. In this part of town no police presence was a good thing—in the eyes of the residents. Kazakov came to a stop where the houses ran out and a field of grass ran away toward the mountains.

The roadside was clogged with marked police vehicles and the M.E.'s wagon. Kazakov pulled in behind them near a gathering crowd, but instead of expensive suits like Bure had worn, these men wore dusty trousers and woolen work shirts with their small white, embroidered felt *ak kalpak* perched on their heads. The women wore scarves and one ancient grandmother even wore the bright skirts and white, ornately wound *el echek* turban of the Kyrgyz hill tribes like a ghost out of time.

Once these people and their Uzbek cousins had been the only people in Fergana. Now, after the influx of people and two hundred years of large families amongst the Russians, they were a minority in their own land and becoming more so every year. To the point where some whispered that they sympathized with Fergana's enemies. So far there'd been no trouble, but bad blood festered and there were even rumors of the Krygyz spying in the mountains for the Ottomans against the Chinese.

Kazakov climbed out to the sound of angry murmurs.

Police tape had been set up, roping off an area in the middle of the field. The wind off the eastern Tian Shan Mountains ripped at the tape and its metal poles. It rippled the grass in a sea of violent gold and green and whipped the clothes of the police and the onlookers. Kazakov pulled his karakul collar tighter. It was colder than normal.

Uniformed police officers kept the people at bay. Kazakov waded out into the brittle grass and it rattled and tugged against his pant legs. The earth was hard underfoot and dust rose with each footfall. At the western edge of the old town rose the five peaks of the great Yekaterina's Mountain turned golden in the setting sun.

The body lay tangled in the tall grass with the backdrop of the snow-covered Tian Shan range. His arm was outstretched as if he reached for them, and his legs were tangled as if he'd been running. He wore dark trousers and a plain white shirt—one that looked as if it had been pressed to impress someone. The red bloom of a gunshot wound burned through the center of his back.

Staying to the edge of the police line, Kazakov circled the scene. The victim was young, with that floppy hair the young men were copying from the foreign musicians. His head was turned to one side and his eyes and mouth were open. Beside him knelt Dr. Khan.

"What do we have?" Kazakov asked as he ducked under the tape and knelt beside the M.E.

"Male. Young. I'd say about eighteen. Single shot to the back. By the look of it I'd say it was a large caliber weapon."

"A fight? A mugging?"

Khan lifted his head from examining a hand. "Nothing under his nails. No bruising of the knuckles. I'd say he was running. By his face, I'd say running for his life. Look at the path he left." He pointed.

It was true. A path of crushed grass led toward the northern edge of the old town. "Any idea who he is?"

"The ID in his wallet says his name's Manas uulu Semetai—Semetai son of Manas."

Semetai Manas, but written in the traditional name structure of the Muslim Kyrgyz. Only the most traditional of the Muslim families held names of that fashion and these were even drawn from the heroes of the great oral epic of the Kyrgyz people. Kazakov nodded, stood, and retraced the victim's path, back toward the old town's weathered, grey strained walls.

The path led right into the maze of streets, as if the victim might have burst from them before being gunned down. Kazakov reached the narrow dirt street and stepped between the buildings. The sunlight disappeared and so did the worst of the wind, though a scuffle of dust blew around his feet.

The dryness meant that footprints were hard to distinguish. Clearly this was a well-used route because the dusty soil showed many scuff marks. There were no doors in the walls of the buildings here: the doors must give out onto the cross street. No window up above either. Windows would look out into the interior courtyards. Inside these buildings were private worlds. Ones that no longer quite meshed with the modern city New Moscow had become. Piles of garbage had been set against the wall to await the irregular pickup. With a foot, he shoved aside the pile of bags and melon rinds and a bright patch of color showed even in the gloom.

Pulling gloves on, Kazakov dug through the sour-sweet rot of melon and the remains of old mutton bones—well chewed by dogs. A blue courier bag lay in the dust and muck but a sweet spice he recognized cut through the rot. He picked up the bag by its strap and gingerly carried it back the way he'd come. Visiting Yekaterina's school would have to wait.

§

In the concrete cavern of his office, Kazakov considered his desk and the Weber case's open cardboard evidence box in the center of the top. It held the girl's clothing including her fluffy pink sweater—probably something the girl kept for special occasions—her identification and the schoolbook. Beside it sat the bag he had found. It fit Yekaterina's mother's description of the girl's notebook bag.

At eight o'clock in the evening the office was empty, though a still-steaming cup of tea on Antonov's desk said that it hadn't been empty long. Crime didn't occur according to schedule.

Beyond the lone window that showed through the glass divider to the hall, night had long fallen and the wind flattened a few snowflakes against the glass. He contemplated all the things that needed to be done in this strange case.

Two young people dead, the blue bag a potential connection between them.

Hands encased in thin rubber gloves, he unzipped the bag and rummaged through it. Its contents included a carefully folded white blouse as if the girl had changed into her pink sweater before she died, suggesting that she had some place special that she was going. There were also a small jar of scented cream reminiscent of church incense and school notebooks with the name Yekaterina Weber printed carefully in the center of the inside of each cover. The outside of the covers had the flower and heart doodles and designs of a typical bored student. He could remember doing something similar himself when he was in school, except his doodles had tended more toward airplanes and guns.

Guns like the one that had killed Semetai Manas.

Just what was a school bag belonging to Yekaterina Weber doing in the old town of Fergana? What was it doing so close to a young man's dead body? Multiple murders didn't usually happen within twenty-four hours of each other. Not in New Moscow, though up in the mountains there might be more violence.

He flipped through the pages of the notebooks. Algebra and history: the destruction of an ancient country. The building of Fergana. The tiny new homeland was pressed like a leaf between the Chinese and the Ottomans who, with their sometime allies, the Anglo-German, were intent on completing their conquest of China. It would fulfill the Ottomans' centuries-old ambition of dominating the world. So far Fergana had stood as a neutral space in the Great Game between the two empires. If the Ottomans were victorious, Fergana wouldn't stand a chance.

But that was tomorrow's problem. For today he needed to figure out who had killed two young people and why.

He had tried to interview the Manas family, but in the closed community of the old town he had wasted three hours before determining that the family had abandoned their last known address. None of their neighbors would talk to him. No one would tell him where they'd gone.

He pulled out Yekaterina's old schoolbook diary found at her murder scene and thumbed through it. Why was it there? Why was her bag at the scene of the boy's murder?

The bag suggested the deaths were connected, but the classroom schedule contained only class assignments. He examined the notes on the day of her death, but there was only mention of a term paper to be researched. In the bottom right corner was a doodle of a heart next to the letter P.

He flipped through the pages again and noted the heart repeated many times, while the letter varied between, P, Y and PT. A code of some kind?

He couldn't say, and turned to the history book. It contained only page after page of the old story of the past diarist Yekaterina's escape with her parents and the founding of the Ferganese homeland. It was almost a fable, a creation myth that let people remember there had been another place, another time when they had been a great and noble people under the great Tsarina Yekaterina who had given them freedom. It gave substance to their dreams and to the fables grandmothers told to their grandchildren.

Of course, a child's schoolbook didn't mention how that same Tzarina had brought destruction upon them all by waking the slumbering Ottoman empire with her armies. Or how she had kept her people enslaved as serfs until the extent of the Ottoman destruction was so great that the whole system supporting her kingdom collapsed and she was forced to take refuge with the common people. That was the uncomfortable truth of their democractic freedom that most people failed to remember.

He went to close the book but something caught his eye. The inside back cover held a simple inscription.

For Yekaterina, my heart.

Love, Semetai.

There was his connection.

That and a pink sweater that a young, infatuated girl would wear to meet her sweetheart.

A chill ran up his back in the stillness of the room. From beyond the detective office came the sounds of life in the rest of the station. But not here. Here on his desk there was only death and destruction caused by young love.

She'd been giddy, her mother had said. Foolish, in her stepfather's words. All the signs of a schoolgirl crush, an infatuation. It was the kind of thing that a father would tease a daughter about.

But an infatuation between a good Orthodox Catholic Russian girl, stepdaughter of a man on the rise in politics, and a boy named Semetai?

That would be a problem. A problem the family would want to fix.

Both families?

Manas uulu Semetai was a name steeped in tribal traditions and there was no love lost between the tribes and the Russian newcomers—not anymore.

The lashes on the girl's back before she was stabbed. Could that be a scourging by an angry family— angry that she had seduced their boy?

Had the Manas family run because they'd killed the girl? And was that why there was such strangeness in the Bure family? Had they done the same in return?

"I need to understand!" He shoved back from his desk, stood, and then stabbed the desk phone with his finger. It buzzed in his ear and then clicked as someone answered.

"Khan?"

"Yes." The calm voice of the M.E. soothed him over the phone. The M.E. would be nearing the end of his shift this evening.

"I need to talk to you. Do you have time?"

There was silence a moment and Kazakov heard the smile. "No. But you will come anyway. I will be here." He hung up.

As Kazakov pulled his coat on, the office door yanked open and Detektiv Chief Inspektor Rostoff pushed into the room. Once they had been friends. They had gone through police training together, but Rostoff had had a free ride because of his family connections. Those same connections had let him rise quickly in rank. Now his large red nose and bleary eyes tracked across the room and settled on Kazakov.

"The others are out? Good. Busy men. Always busy. I like to see that." Rostoff was a bear of a man, in the old Russian style, with a heavy coat and fur hat in winter. In the fall it was just the coat that reeked of too much sweat leached into old wool. Rostoff pulled his gloves off and strode through the desks to Kazakov.

"Good man." He scanned the evidence on the desk. "A case. You are busy? Yes?" He pounded Kazakov's shoulder and then hitched a leg over the corner of a neighboring desk and sat.

Rostoff never showed his face in the detective section and certainly not at this hour. He was too busy rubbing shoulders with the big wigs in the justice department. That he was here now was a worry.

Rostoff grinned a big yellow smile. "My dear Kazakov. Look at the hour."

Kazakov did. Eight-forty pm. He had worked later many times. The question was what or who had brought Rostoff here.

"You are a good man. You work hard, my old friend. Maybe sometimes you work too hard."

Kazakov went cold as Rostoff pointedly scanned the evidence again, then casually picked up the diary, the school schedule and bag and dropped them in the cardboard evidence box.

"This case, it has you worried, yes? I can tell by the look in your eyes. Would it surprise you that it has others worried, too? Maybe you should not worry so much. Maybe sometimes you should let things go. Yes?" His yellow smile broadened as he settled the box top in place. "You see? Not so difficult."

Frozen, Kazakov just looked at him. What could he do that would not bring the weight of Rostoff's sanctions down on him? What could he say? "It's a double murder. Since when do we let such things go?"

Rostoff said nothing but his thick lips curved in a semblance of a dismissive smile.

Clenching his fists, Kazakov turned his back on the other man and headed for the door.

§

Rostoff might have handed down an official decree, but that didn't mean Kazakov had to listen. It was a double murder. A murder of children. Surely to God, that meant something.

The M.E.'s offices sat in the basement of the Our Lady Yekaterina Hospital. It was a large, four-story building built with a fountain and garden in the front that briefly, in the springtime, could be called beautiful. But summer brought the winds off the mountains that drank the water from the fountain and leached the trees to the color of dust. In October, the fountain was brown with leaves. In November the snow would be falling. Kazakov left his sedan in the street-lit parking lot and strode through the stand of half-barren, night-bound trees under the half-grown moon. They were the tallest in Fergana—maples while in most of the city it was generally aspen that survived the wind and snow of the winter. The red leaves were a particular treat in a town built mainly of concrete, and he liked the way they shuffled around his feet. Almost like snow, without the cold and the shoveling.

He bypassed the hospital's well-lit main door and went down a shadowed set of concrete stairs to one side of the structure. A metal door was locked, but he knocked and the door buzzed. He pushed inside into the stomach-clenching smells of blood and guts and formaldehyde. The receptionist nodded him through.

If Khalil Khan was busy, he had made time for Kazakov. He sat behind a small, scarred wooden desk in a small office as if he was waiting. He had two files closed before him on the desk and nodded Kazakov into the lone chair across from him. Behind Khan the wall was lined with books.

"Tell me what I don't know," Kazakov asked.

"The boy was killed with an antique rifle. The bullet was of a type only used for some of the old Chinese makes." He looked at his hands and let the news hang in the air. "It's the kind the Kyrgyz use for hunting. They trade for them at the markets on the other side of the mountains—when the Ottomans and Chinese aren't fighting."

"Any likelihood of a Russian getting their hands on such a weapon?" Given Khan was Kyrgyz he would have an insight into such things.

Khan pursed his lips and shrugged. "Maybe. It might be possible—from police evidence lockers perhaps, but otherwise unlikely. They aren't licensed and they're kept hidden. The Kyrgyz take their weapons seriously. These things are almost family heirlooms— reminders of a time before the Russians took over and regulated everything."

He said it carefully, no inflection in his voice. It must be difficult for a descendent of those tribal people to see how their world had become a Russian country.

"So, what you're saying is that Semetai Manas was likely killed by his own people."

Khan didn't say anything, only met his gaze.

"You know something," Kazakov said softly.

Khan shook his head. "Not know. At least not know-as-evidence know. But there are things in this culture, just as in yours. The sense of proper. The sense of place and the need for continuity of a people. You cannot let anything get in the way of that. Of the blood."

A sick feeling settled in the pit of Kazakov's stomach. Such pride and sense of people ran strong in Russians too. It was bred into them. It was fed in schools with books such as Yekaterina's diary and by the state in the names of hospitals and parks and streets and mountains that bore different names depending on who you spoke to.

"The girl. The lashes."

Khan nodded. "They were deep. Made with rage. There were also deep bruises on her neck and shoulders. I'd say she was throttled in anger, then held down for the lashing before she was stabbed. Whoever did it buried the hilt of the knife deep in her. The edges of the wound were deeply torn."

The air was too close, the stench of death too strong as Kazakov heaved himself up out of the chair.

"One more thing," Khan said. "She was pregnant."

Feeling momentarily drunk, Kazakov nodded. "How far along?"

"First trimester." Khan looked away at his desk and shook his head.

"Thank you."

Kazakov left the office feeling old and useless and climbed the stairs to the parking lot.

A gust of mountain wind caught him and he staggered and thought he might be ill. Instead he turned his back on the lights illuminating Yekaterina's mountain and fumbled for the lighter and the lone cigarette he kept in his wallet. Shielding them against the wind he lit the cigarette and inhaled the warm acrid tar only to let it out in a long belch of smoke.

The wind tore it away and the moonlight caught on the Tian Shan Mountains that loomed white but no longer so high. No longer so remote. With a sigh, he stubbed the cigarette out and headed for his car. He would need to be very careful or he could light a fire that would ignite his country. There was already too much division between Fergana's Russians and the people whose country the Russians had occupied.

War had found a new way across the mountains.

To read more of *After Yekaterina,* look for it at your favorite bookseller in March 2017.

* 9 7 8 1 9 2 7 7 5 3 6 5 1 *